RJ – Boy Detective

Books 1 - 8

PJ Ryan

Contents

"RJ - Boy Detective" is a short story series for children ages 9-12 with the remaining titles to be published on a regular basis. Each title can be read on its own.

I'd really love to hear from you!

I very much appreciate your reviews and comments so thank you in advance for taking a moment to leave one for "RJ - Boy Detective Books 1-8."

You can join RJ's fun Facebook page for young detectives here:

http://www.facebook.com/RJBoyDetective

Sincerely,
PJ Ryan

All bundled sets are also available in paperback from Amazon. Check the author page here for the complete listing:

http://pjryanbooks.com/

Current series:

RJ – Boy Detective

Rebekah – Girl Detective

Mouse's Secret Club

Rebekah, Mouse & RJ: Special Editions

Additionally several PJ Ryan titles are now available as audiobooks and you can also find those listed at the page above.

RJ – Boy Detective #1

The Mysterious Crate

PJ Ryan

RJ – Boy Detective #1:

The Mysterious Crate

Chapter 1

"The best part about living in a high-rise apartment building, is all of the suspicious characters," RJ announced into the phone as he stood beside the tall window that looked out over the city. He was in his living room, talking to his younger cousin Rebekah who had called as usual for some advice on solving a mystery.

"But isn't a little crowded?" Rebekah asked as politely as she could. She was more of a small town girl, but RJ was a city boy through and through.

"Crowds just make everything more fun," RJ insisted with a slight nod of his head. "I'm looking forward to having the chance to explore the city. Since I turned twelve my parents let me get my very own subway pass."

"Wow, that's pretty great!" Rebekah said. "Don't forget to fill me in on all your adventures!"

"I will," RJ agreed. "I'm about to head out on a mission right now actually."

"Good luck!" Rebekah said as she hung up. RJ opened his closet door and looked over his wide selection of detective hats. Each day he could choose a different color, but they were all about the same shape and size. Once he picked his hat he tucked it on top of his red hair.

"RJ are you going now?" his mother called out as he stepped out of his room.

"Yes Mom, I'll be back before dinner," he called back as he walked down the hall.

RJ took the elevator down to the second floor. While he rode down in the elevator, he thought about the people he knew on each floor. His parents were the landlords of the building, and so he had the chance to meet just about every tenant that moved in.

These were the suspicious characters that he was telling Rebekah about. Like Mrs. Listern, who always put her garbage in the chute at exactly 9:58 every night. Never 9:59, never 9:57, always 9:58. Now if that wasn't suspicious then RJ didn't know what was. Of course old Mr. Helmsley was the strangest. He never ever opened his door. If a package was delivered he would speak through the door. If something needed to be signed he would tell them to slide it under the door. There were a few other kids in the building, but not many. The only one that RJ really spent any time with was Joey, and that was not exactly by choice. Joey's mom worked late, so after school RJ would look after him until she got home. He was only eight but he was a cool kid just the same. RJ had solved a few mysteries about different people in the building, but most of the time they turned out to be boring explanations. He'd yet to find a true mystery to solve, but he knew there was one waiting for him.

Chapter 2

When RJ went to meet Joey's bus after school, he found the boy was looking pretty down.

"What's wrong?" RJ asked him with a frown.

"Nothing," Joey sighed as he trudged toward the building. RJ followed behind him. He could tell by the slump of his shoulders and the way that he was dragging his book bag on the ground that there was definitely something wrong.

"Is there a kid at school giving you a hard time?" RJ asked with a frown. "If someone's being mean to you, I can have a talk with them," RJ promised.

"Really?" Joey perked up slightly.

"Of course, we have to stick together," he gave Joey's shoulder a light pat.

"Thanks," Joey said, but he shook his head. "It's not that. It's just this," he stopped in the middle of the sidewalk and unzipped his book bag. He pulled out a piece of paper with a big red letter F on it.

"Oh no," RJ frowned. "Did you fail a test?"

"Yup," Joey sighed. "Mom is not going to be happy."

"Don't worry," RJ assured him. "We'll go over it and figure out what went wrong."

"Really?" Joey asked happily.

"Of course," RJ nodded. "Getting a bad grade just means that you need to study more, it doesn't mean that you did anything wrong. So we'll figure it out together."

When they returned to Joey's apartment they looked over his homework together. Once Joey got the hang of it, they were free to explore the city. There was a park not far from the apartment building that the boys liked to go to in the afternoon.

"Where are you two off to?" Hensely, the doorman asked as he held the door open for bother of them. Hensely always kept an eye on RJ and Joey. In fact, when RJ needed to go somewhere in the city that he knew he shouldn't go to alone, Hensely would usually tag along with him. He was in his late sixties, and had thin gray eyebrows. His eyes were dark brown, and his smile was nearly hidden by a bushy gray mustache. Even though there was quite a big age difference between them, RJ still considered him one of his best friends.

"Just to the park," RJ promised.

"No mysteries today?" Hensely asked with surprise.

"No mystery," RJ replied firmly.

"Alright, have fun. Remember, be back here before it gets dark, okay?" he looked both boys in the eyes. "And stick together."

'We always do," Joey promised as they set off in that direction of the park.

Chapter 3

After they played for a while and the sun was beginning to set, RJ called out to Joey.

"Time to go. Your Mom will be home soon."

Joey was shooting some hoops on the basketball court.

"Just one more?" he begged.

"Alright," RJ nodded. "But hurry up because I don't want your Mom to worry about where we are."

"It was so simple for him to just toss the ball into the hoop and listen to the sound of the swish as it fell through the net. But instead he decided that he needed to try to make a trick shot. He turned around and tossed the ball up over his head. The ball bounced off the edge of the rim, which was pretty impressive considering that Joey wasn't even looking at the basket. But the ball landed in the grass instead of on the court and it began to roll away.

"Grab it!" RJ shouted as they began to chase after it. It was pretty clear that the ball was much faster than they were as it rolled down the grassy hill. Now RJ could see it nearing a small stream that cut through the park. He knew if it landed in there, they would not likely be able to get it back. So he ran as fast as he could and passed right by Joey. When he reached the ball he managed to snatch it up before it could roll into the water.

"Oh good you got it," Joey said with a sigh of relief. The ball didn't belong to him, but one of the older kids on the playground and if Joey had lost it, he would not have been allowed anywhere near the basketball court ever again. It had taken them so long to retrieve the ball that the sun had fully set by the time they began walking back toward the apartments.

"Stay close to me," RJ commanded. He loved the city, but it was always good to be cautious anywhere at night. As they walked beside the sky scraper buildings and were jostled by the ever-busy people of the city, RJ hoped that Joey's mom hadn't made it home yet. She was usually pretty nice, but if she found out that he had Joey out in the city after dark, she would not be happy about it at all. As they reached the front entrance of the apartment complex RJ halted suddenly when he saw a shadow across the front of the building. He grabbed Joey's shoulder and tugged him backward behind a large trash can. As the man walked toward the building, RJ recognized who he was. He was the new tenant in 3B. RJ had helped him move some boxes from the moving truck into the elevator on the day he moved in. He had thought he was kind of strange then too. But now he looked very strange, because he was trying to carry a very large crate. RJ had a strange feeling. He was sure that the man was trying to hide something, which meant, it could be something dangerous.

"Joey, get down!" RJ said sharply as the man carrying the crate walked right past them. Joey ducked down behind the large trash can they were trying to hide behind. RJ's hat was sticking up above it. Luckily the man who was carrying the crate couldn't see over it, so he didn't notice the two hiding.

"What do you think he has in there?" RJ asked with narrowed eyes. "I bet it's something illegal."

"Illegal?" Joey asked as he looked up at RJ nervously.

"Against the law," RJ explained. "Why else would he be sneaking around with it?"

"Maybe, he's afraid someone will steal it," Joey suggested with a half-shrug. "Maybe he thinks if someone sees him with it, they will want to know what's in the crate so badly that they just have to look inside. Then they will follow after him and steal the crate and pry it open and-"

"Joey," RJ groaned and followed it with a sigh. Joey had the type of mind that just kept going and going. It was hard to keep up with what he was saying when he never paused for a breath.

"I'm just saying maybe," Joey said with a frown.

"Shh," RJ insisted as the man walked through the entrance of the apartment building. It was not an easy feat either. He nearly dropped the crate as he tried to open the door and carry it through at the same time.

"See," RJ hissed. "If he wasn't doing something wrong then he wouldn't have waited until after Hensely's shift was over. Why would anyone want to carry something that large by himself?"

Joey nodded silently as they both watched the door close.

"So what's in it?" Joey wondered, his eyes wide.

"That's what we need to find out," RJ said with determination.

"But how?" Joey shook his head. "It's not like he's going to let us have a look."

"Well then," RJ smirked slightly as he glanced in Joey's direction. "I guess we shouldn't ask."

Chapter 4

When RJ and Joey got back to Joey's apartment they were both relieved to find that Joey's mom hadn't made it home yet. At least they wouldn't have to explain why they were late. Together they sat down at the kitchen table. RJ whipped out his cell phone which had a special app for taking notes. He tapped out a quick note.

Mystery crate
What's inside?
How do we find out?

"These are the questions that we need to answer," RJ said and tapped lightly at his chin. "So we need a plan. How are we going to find out what's inside of the crate?"

"Well, do you have some of those cool x-ray glasses that I've seen in the movies," Joey said eagerly.

"No," RJ frowned.

"Well do you know a secret passageway into his apartment?" Joey said hopefully.

"No," RJ shook his head.

"Well what kind of detective are you, RJ?" Joey said with annoyance.

"I have a magnifying glass," RJ said quickly and whipped it out of the large pocket of his jacket.

"Well maybe we can use it to look through the peephole," Joey rolled his eyes.

"That's it!" RJ announced with a snap of his fingers.

"That's what?" Joey asked with confusion.

"The door. All we need to do is figure out how to get through the door. How can he hide a crate that big in a little one bedroom apartment?" he asked with a growing smile.

"Right," Joey said slowly. "But how do we get through the door? Oh I know!" he gasped with excitement. "Do you have some of that gum that you can chew up and stick to the door and it blows a hole in it and the door opens and then you go inside-"

"Joey!" RJ snapped and then shook his head. "I don't have any of that. But we don't need that. A good detective uses this," he tapped the side of his head lightly.

"Oh, is it like a boomerang hat, or a hat with super powers?" Joey said hopefully.

"No Joey," RJ sighed. "I'm talking about my head, my brain. A good detective has to use his smarts to solve a mystery," he said firmly.

"Oh," Joey said with clear disappointment. "I guess that's good too. So what does your brain tell you?" he asked.

"It tells me that all we have to do is get Mr. Porter to open the door," RJ said with a slow smile.

"But he won't just open his door if he's trying to hide something," Joey pointed out with a frown.

"He will if it's the landlord's son," RJ said with confidence. 'He won't want to seem suspicious. We can pretend we're selling something for school. Like cookies or candy or something."

"That's a good idea!" Joey agreed.

"Okay, first thing tomorrow afternoon we're going to get inside of that apartment," RJ said with determination.

Chapter 5

The next afternoon RJ met Joey's bus with a school fundraiser pamphlet that he had saved from the year before.

"This is going to get us in the door," RJ said firmly. Joey looked a little skeptical but he nodded.

"We'll give it a shot," he agreed. They dropped off Joey's book bag at his apartment and then rode the elevator to the third floor. Mr. Porter's apartment was at the end of a long hallway. When they reached it, RJ frowned.

"Now Joey, remember we need to be very careful, just in case Mr. Porter is up to something dangerous," he said sternly.

"I know, I know," Joey nodded. Then he reached forward and knocked hard on the door. No one answered at first. So RJ took a turn knocking. Finally they heard the lock release, and the door swung slightly open.

"What is it?" Mr. Porter asked impatiently.

"Hi there," RJ smiled at him charmingly. "Remember me?"

"Sure, RJ right?" Mr. Porter asked with annoyance. "What do you kids want?"

RJ opened his mouth to explain, but he couldn't say a single word, before Joey started talking.

"Hi Mr. Porter, I'm Joey. I live here too. It's nice to meet you. My school is trying to raise money by selling these wonderful items. Please take some time to look through the brochure. We'll be using the money to buy things for the school, like music equipment, sports equipment, building supplies, and-"

"Wow!" Mr. Porter said as his eyes widened. "Would you slow down for just a minute kid?" he asked, Joey's fast talking making him knit his eyebrows with confusion.

Joey didn't slow down in the least, he just continued rattling on while RJ grimaced and shook his head.

"So there are many things you could choose from. Wrapping paper, cookies, candy, they're all very quality items, and would make great gifts. I mean if you wanted to give a gift. If you have someone to give a gift to. But if you don't that's okay too, because you could give a gift to yourself. Which is always good. Sometimes I wrap things up and hide them in my room, so then when I find them, I'm all surprised and happy because I got a gift!"

"Joey!" RJ snapped and widened his eyes.

"Enough, enough," Mr. Porter sighed and lifted his hands into the air. "If I buy something will you kids leave me alone?" he asked with one raised eyebrow.

"Sure," Joey said with a sweet smile.

"Absolutely," RJ agreed, amazed that Joey's relentless speech had actually worked.

"Just let me get my checkbook," Mr. Porter said and started to turn away from the door. RJ saw his opportunity and stuck his foot in the opening of the door. Then he stepped all the way in behind Mr. Porter.

Chapter 6

"I didn't say that you could come in," Mr. Porter growled as he rummaged through a drawer in the table beside the door.

"Sorry, I thought you had," RJ said quickly. He observed as much of the apartment as he could see. Everything looked pretty normal. There were paintings on the wall, an overstuffed couch and a nice coffee table with a few scratches and smudges. There was a rather odd smell in the apartment though. RJ couldn't quite place it. It didn't smell like anything dangerous though.

"Well next time ask," Mr. Porter said sharply as Joey stepped in behind RJ.

"Yes sir, of course," RJ nodded and then bounced from one foot to the other. "The thing is, I really was hoping that I might be able to use your bathroom. I don't know if I can make it to my apartment!" he winced as if he was already about to burst.

"Are you serious?" Mr. Porter gasped with irritation. Then he looked at RJ. He must have remembered that he was the son of the landlord, because he tried to speak more nicely to him.

"Alright, but please just make it quick. I really have things to do and you kids have interrupted me."

"So sorry," RJ said quickly as Mr. Porter pointed down the hallway in the direction of the bathroom.

"Just use the bathroom and come right back," Mr. Porter said sternly. RJ smirked a little. Now he was sure that Mr. Porter was hiding something. Otherwise why would he be so nervous about RJ using the bathroom? Of course RJ did not really have to go to the bathroom. He just wanted to see more of the apartment. He had yet to see the large crate, but he knew it had to be there somewhere. He walked toward the bathroom.

"So who do I make this out to?" Mr. Porter asked when he found his check book.

"That's a funny story actually," Joey said as he did his best to distract Mr. Porter. "You see our school actually has two names. It used to be Millersville Grade School then it changed to Millersville Community Grade School. Then they changed it back. I mean we kept having to change our school t-shirts because they couldn't get the name right. So-"

"Stop!" Mr. Porter growled and threw his check book down on the table. "I'll just use cash to pay for it."

While Joey was explaining to Mr. Porter how he had learned how to count and add money and his possible future career as an accountant, RJ hit pay dirt. The bedroom door was right next to the bathroom. It was closed, but not quite all the way. RJ ducked into the bathroom and turned on the sink so that Mr. Porter would think he was still washing his hands. Then he nudged the bedroom door open. There it was. The large crate was wedged between the bed and the wall and half-covered with a blanket. RJ wanted to rush in and open up the crate, but he knew he didn't have enough time. He could hear Joey still stalling over the payment. The water in the bathroom had been running for some time. RJ noticed that the blanket was not covering a label on the crate. He thought maybe that would give him a clue or some evidence. Luckily he had his spy camera with him. His spy camera was a camera that he wore on a strap around his arm underneath his sleeve. This let him hide the camera quickly.

Using his trusty spy camera RJ hung his arm through the door of the bedroom, and snapped a few wild pictures. He could only hope that one of them captured the label that was on the front of the crate. Then he slid the camera back under his sleeve. He ducked quickly back into the bathroom and turned the water off, then walked back down the hall to the living room. His blue eyes were wide as the man turned to face him with a few dollars in his hand.

"Here," he said gruffly. "I guess this should cover it, right? I mean how much do cookies cost?"

"It's perfect," RJ said with a polite smile. "Thanks so much for supporting our school."

"Right, right, of course," Mr. Porter said dismissively. "Now boys," he said in a stern tone. "I don't want you coming back here asking me to buy anything else, understand?" he gave them both a look of warning.

"Understood," RJ nodded sharply.

"I'm a very busy man," Mr. Porter continued. "And I like my privacy. So no more knocking on my door, hm?" he looked directly at RJ. "Or I will discuss this with your parents."

RJ winced as he knew that if Mr. Porter brought this up with his parents they would inform him that he was not part of any fund raiser. Not only would Mr. Porter be suspicious, but his parents would certainly ground him for making up such a story.

"No problem Mr. Porter," RJ assured him. "We won't be back!"

Chapter 7

As soon as they got back to Joey's apartment, RJ pulled out his camera. He expanded the picture so that he could see the writing on the label.

"Jungle Supplies," RJ read off of the label with a frown of confusion. "What in the world could the jungle have to do with the crate?" he sighed with disappointment. He had hoped that the clue would give him a little more information.

"Maybe he's a spy," Joey suggested with wide eyes. "Maybe those are his spy tools in the crate. Then he would put a pretend label on it to confuse us."

"No, I don't think he's a spy," RJ shook his head and then tugged on the brim of his detective's hat. "I think he's hiding something very dangerous. Something that has something to do with the jungle!"

"Oh no," Joey gasped and slid his chair back across the kitchen floor. "You don't think it's snakes, do you? Maybe he's smuggling jungle snakes! Oh I don't like snakes. This one time I was walking down the street and there was this big black snake-"

"Joey," RJ said sharply. "We don't know that it's snakes. We don't know what it is at all. But I can tell you this much, nothing from the jungle belongs in the city."

"But how are we going to figure it out now?" Joey asked with a frown. "Mr. Porter told us not to come back."

"We'll just have to wait until he's out," RJ explained. "And sneak in."

"You mean break in?" Joey asked with surprise. "Now that's doing something illegal."

"Good point," RJ frowned. He considered calling his cousin Rebekah. She always had adventurous ways to solve her mysteries. But she was usually the one asking him for advice.

"It wouldn't be good to break in," he finally agreed. "But if he let us in again, then it would be just fine."

"How would he let us in again?" Joey asked feeling even more confused.

"Meet me first thing tomorrow morning at my apartment," RJ declared with a smirk. "And I'll show you."

Chapter 8

The next morning was Saturday so they didn't have to go to school. RJ was still up early. He waited until his father was out of the apartment and then he found his old tool box. He also found a notice that he had printed off of the computer in the past. It was a notice to all tenants that there was a water leak somewhere in the building, and that all plumbing would have to be checked. Of course that had happened two years before. RJ just changed the date on the notice and printed it out. Then he picked up the tool box. When he opened the front door of his apartment, he found Joey standing there.

"What is that for?" he asked as he pointed to the toolbox.

"Today we're going to be plumbers," RJ grinned.

"Uh," Joey scratched his head and frowned. "Do you even know what a wrench is?"

"Sure," RJ said sternly. "It's one of these," he pointed into the tool box. "With the handles."

"Great," Joey raised his eyebrows. "I don't think that this is going to work."

"It's worth a try," RJ said sternly. "All I need is a little more time inside of the apartment and then we will find out what's inside of the crate."

"Okay," Joey nodded. "If you say so RJ."

They both walked to the elevator and rode it up to the third floor. When they walked near Mr. Porter's apartment, they were met with a surprise. He was outside of it, carrying a bag of garbage. He was headed down to the end of the hall to drop it off. RJ saw his chance, as the front door of Mr. Porter's apartment was still open. He ducked inside, with Joey right behind him. Now Mr. Porter wouldn't be able to close and lock the door on them.

"Hey!" Mr. Porter shouted when he saw them disappear into his apartment. "What are you doing in here?" he demanded, his cheeks red with anger.

"Oh sorry Mr. Porter," RJ said nervously as he held up the notice. "My Dad asked me to check out your sink and toilet for a water leak."

"Why isn't the maintenance man or your Dad doing it?" Mr. Porter asked suspiciously.

"There are so many apartments," RJ explained. "Since it's a Saturday my Dad asked me to help out. But if you'd rather I go get him-" RJ started to say. It worked like a charm. As RJ suspected Mr. Porter didn't want to risk the landlord figuring out what he was up to.

"Fine just make it fast," Mr. Porter grumbled. "And just go into the bathroom and the kitchen, there's nothing else to check."

"Yes sir," RJ said. He and Joey started walking toward the bathroom. They heard Mr. Porter turn on the television. When RJ heard that he gave the tool box to Joey.

"Just go in the bathroom and bang one of those tools on something metal. Make it sound like you're doing something," RJ whispered. "I'll go in the bedroom and see what's in that crate."

"Alright," Joey said with a grin. He was having fun. While Joey started banging on the pipes with a wrench, RJ ducked into the bedroom. A second later, Mr. Porter opened the door.

"What are you doing in here?" he roared. Joey came running out of the bathroom, his eyes wide with fear.

"Uh, sorry I thought this was the bathroom-" RJ started to explain as he glanced at the crate.

"No, enough with the lying," Mr. Porter said firmly. "No one bangs on pipes," he said sternly. "You two weren't sent here by your father RJ. So why are you two bothering me?"

He marched RJ and Joey back out into the living room. "Whatever it is you think you're doing, it has to stop. I could tell the police about this you know!"

"Sure, and we could tell them about what you have in that crate," RJ countered, his eyes narrowed.

"Is that really what all this was about?" Mr. Porter asked with a shake of his head. "All you boys wanted to know was what was in that crate?" he chuckled, but the sound wasn't quite normal. It was a little bit scary.

Chapter 9

"No we don't need to know," Joey said quickly and started to back up.

"No, you two were spying on me. Obviously you want to know what's in the crate. Let me ask you this, what do you think is in it?"

RJ shrugged as he eyed Mr. Porter suspiciously. "Maybe something illegal," he said bravely.

"Illegal?" Mr. Porter laughed loudly. "Is that what you really think?"

"Well, why else would you be sneaking it into the apartment?" RJ asked with more determination.

"Well it's not technically illegal," Mr. Porter explained. "But it is something that most landlords don't want to know about. So if I show you, you boys have to promise that this will be our secret."

RJ shook his head slowly. "My parents are the landlords Mr. Porter. If you have something in that crate that they wouldn't like, I'm certainly going to tell them."

Mr. Porter pursed his lips for a moment, and then cast a glance RJ's direction. "I think if you see what's inside, you might just change your mind."

"Fine, show us," Joey requested. He just couldn't wait any longer.

Mr. Porter walked over to the crate. He loosened the wooden top. Then he lifted the top off of the crate. At first nothing happened. Then they saw a long brown tail curl its way over the side of the box.

"What is that?" RJ asked with surprise. Before Mr. Porter could speak, the crate began to make some very strange sounds. It chattered. It shook. It even shrieked. Joey jumped behind RJ. RJ stared at the box with wide horrified eyes.

"Just what are you hiding in there Mr. Porter?" he asked, his voice shaking as he spoke.

"Take a look," Mr. Porter laughed. RJ's mind filled with some horrible things. Little gremlins clamoring to get out. An entire flock of bats. Or maybe even something much worse. He really didn't want to look inside but he had to know what it was. He stepped closer to the edge of the crate and peered over the edge. A pair of big round eyes peered right back at him.

"Th-that's a monkey!" RJ declared with surprise. "You've got a monkey in that crate!"

Mr. Porter held out his hands to the monkey, who happily climbed up and out of the crate. He grabbed on to Mr. Porter's shoulders and grinned at the two boys. RJ and Joey were speechless as they stared at the monkey who was making faces at Mr. Porter.

"He's not usually in the crate," Mr. Porter explained. "I just put him in there when I move him, or when someone drops by."

"He's so cute," Joey said with a gasp as the monkey grinned at him. "What's his name?"

"Theodore," Mr. Porter replied and patted the top of the monkey's head. "He's my best friend."

"But he's a monkey," RJ pointed out, still feeling a little uneasy.

"Sure he is," Mr. Porter nodded. "But he's also a great listener. He likes to play checkers."

"He plays checkers with you?" Joey laughed. "That's amazing!"

Mr. Porter smiled and nodded. Then he looked at RJ. "So now you know my big secret RJ," he said quietly. "It's up to you if you are going to keep it."

RJ frowned. He knew that his parents probably wouldn't allow Mr. Porter to keep his monkey, but he thought it was really cool to have a monkey in the building!

"Well, as long as you don't let him loose, and he's well trained, I don't think I need to tell."

"Thanks," Mr. Porter said with a sigh of relief. "I've had to move so many times. I just can't live where Theodore can't live with me. I paid extra to have a pet in the apartment, I just didn't say that it was a monkey. So that is why I had to sneak him in at night when no one was around."

"Don't worry," Joey said with a smile as he waved his hand at the monkey. "Your secret is safe with us."

Chapter 10

When RJ got home that night he thought about Theodore and Mr. Porter. He knew that it was never good to lie, but he understood why Mr. Porter did not want to lose his friend.

"Good night RJ," his father called when he checked in on him.

"Good night Dad," RJ called back. Before his father shut the door, RJ spoke up. "Dad, can you do me a favor?"

"What is it?" his father asked as he paused in the doorway.

"Do you think you could pick up some extra bananas tomorrow?" RJ asked hopefully.

"Sure," his father nodded and closed the door to his bedroom. RJ fell asleep dreaming of having a game of checkers with Theodore.

RJ – Boy Detective #2:

Vampire Hunting

Chapter 1

RJ was just sitting down with his latest scary novel. He was looking forward to getting into the story and discovering who was responsible for the disappearing gravestones. As he flipped through the pages he had already read, he heard a strange sound. It was a distant sound, too far away to be coming from his apartment. It was very loud, but muffled, making it hard to tell what it was and where it was coming from. It was a repetitive sound.

He stood up from his chair and walked out of his bedroom and into the living room. His mother and father were out doing their monthly evaluations with the tenants, checking to see if everything was in working order and whether there were repairs needed anywhere in the building.

He was alone in the apartment. There shouldn't have been anything making any noise, except for him. No matter where he walked in the apartment, the kitchen, his parents' bedroom, the study, even the bathroom, he could still hear the noise. But it was still at a distance. So he decided to see if he could hear it in the hallway.

He snatched his hat off of the hat rack he hung it on by the door and pulled it down tightly on his head. He always wore his detective's hat when there was a mystery afoot. He had a wide assortment of them to choose from in different colors.

As he stepped out into the hallway he listened very closely. He heard Mrs. Warbush's washing machine churning. He heard Mr. Albert's television blaring. He heard the Chomski twins bouncing a ball back and forth. There was plenty of noise with so many neighbors, but beyond all of this noise he heard that thumping.

He looked up at the ceiling as it seemed to be coming from above his head. Could it be something on the roof? As a rule he was not allowed on the roof alone, but he had occasionally broken that rule. Only for the sake of solving a mystery. This did seem like a mystery to him.

Chapter 2

He began walking toward the stairwell that led to the roof. It was all the way at the end of the green carpeted hallway. As he walked past Mrs. Warbush's apartment he heard her dryer turn on. As he walked past Mr. Albert's apartment he heard him change the channel from history to game shows. As he walked past the Chomski apartment, he heard the twins' mother insisting they not play ball in the apartment. All of these things were things he expected to hear when walking down the hallway.

When he stepped into the stairwell, the thumping sound became a little louder. Every ounce of RJ's being was telling him that something extraordinary was about to occur.

As he stood in the stairwell, he could hear both the muffled thumping sound and something else. Something like scraping against the steps leading up to where he was standing. His muscles got so tight that he couldn't even bring himself to turn around. He had no idea what was creeping up behind him.

He was usually very brave in such circumstances, but this time he was nervous. When he felt long skinny fingers grasp his shoulder tightly he let out a wild yelp and spun around to face whoever was touching him.

"Heya RJ!" Joey declared with an impish smile. Joey was a young neighbor that RJ often kept track of after school and during the summer.

"Joey you scared me!" RJ gasped out and put his hand against the wall to steady himself. "Er, I mean you shouldn't sneak up on people. Of course I wasn't actually scared, but I could have been scared if I was someone else," he quirked a brow, as he felt a little confused by his own words.

"Sorry," Joey squeaked out. "Look I got new shoes!" he pointed at his shoes which were actually cleats. "I get to play soccer now!"

RJ shook his head as he rested all of his weight on the wall. That explained the scraping sound he had heard. "Good for you," he said. "Maybe we can kick the ball around at the park sometime. But right now I've got a mystery to solve."

"A mystery?" Joey piped up. "Can I help? You know I'm really good at helping. Please RJ can I help?" he smiled as innocently as he could.

"Joey, I don't think that's a good idea," RJ began to say firmly. He was going up to the roof which was no place for a kid, but before he could explain, his hand seemed to sink into the wall. It happened so fast that RJ couldn't keep his balance.

"Ah!" he cried out as he fell right over and landed half in the stairwell and half inside of the wall.

Chapter 3

"RJ?" Joey gasped as he looked down at his friend. "Did you just break the wall? You're going to be in so much trouble!"

"No," RJ sputtered as he tried to free his face of the dust that was gathered on the floor of the inside of the wall. "There's some kind of door here," he said as he sat up slowly. He was still half inside and half outside of the wall.

"Where did that come from?" Joey asked, looking very puzzled.

"I don't know," RJ admitted as he crawled out of the wall and peered closely at the door. He pulled out his magnifying glass, a special gift from his cousin Rebekah, and peered at the door. There was no sign of hinges. The door had a perfect seal. When it was closed, it could not be seen. Only someone who knew it was there would know to push on the wall and open it.

"What do you think is in there?" Joey asked as he peered curiously into the hidden hallway.

"I'm not sure," RJ said quietly. "I want to find out though. Let's take a look," he suggested, and then paused a moment. "Well, if you don't think it's too scary?"

"No, of course not," Joey shook his head firmly. "I can't wait to see what's inside. Let's go!"

RJ stepped cautiously into the hallway. As he walked, he could hear the floorboards creaking beneath his feet. The hallway was only about as wide as his elbows could stretch. It was filled with cobwebs and dust, and not much else. He wondered why anyone would have built it, or hidden it, in the first place. As he neared the end of the hallway he saw something standing out against the darkness. It was a wooden ladder propped up against the wall.

"Wow," Joey said from behind RJ. "Do you think it's a ghost ladder?"

"A what?" RJ asked with confusion.

"You know, a ladder that used to be a real ladder, but now it's a ghost ladder," Joey explained with an eager smile, as if he really believed every word he was speaking.

"A ghost ladder?" RJ said dismissively. "Of course it's not a ghost ladder. Ladders can't be ghosts."

"Just because you've never seen one, doesn't mean they're not real," Joey pointed out with a frown.

"Uh, no they're not real," RJ insisted, but he was too curious about the ladder to continue to argue. He crept slowly closer to it. All the dust in the hallway made it a little difficult to see, even with the flashlight shining down the hallway. When he shined the light directly on the ladder, he could see a little more detail.

The ladder looked just as old and untouched as the hallway did. It was difficult to tell if anyone had been there in many years. RJ peered up the ladder, following each rung higher and higher. He could see that it led to a trap door in the ceiling, but he had no idea what might be beyond that door.

As he put his foot on the bottom rung of the latter he took a deep breath and did his best to appear very brave. Joey was right behind him bouncing from one foot to the other.

"What do you see, what do you see?" he asked eagerly.

"Shh," RJ hissed over his shoulder. Then he climbed up the next rung on the ladder. As he got higher on the ladder the dust cleared a little. There was a small square trap door in the ceiling of the hallway. It was right above the top rung of the ladder. When RJ reached the top rung he stretched his fingers out to touch the trap door. It creaked the moment he touched it.

He could hear the thumping now very loudly. It was definitely coming from beyond that door. From below him he heard Joey's shrill voice calling out to him. "Can I climb up now? Can I climb up now please?" he begged.

"Shh!" RJ hissed again over his shoulder. "Would you please be quiet? You're going to make me fall off of this ladder if you keep it up," RJ warned with annoyance. He turned back to the door and frowned. He knew whatever had been making the strange noise was on the other side of that door. He just wasn't sure if he was ready to find out what it was.

Since Joey was below, watching his every move, he wasn't left with much of a choice. He didn't want the kid to think that he wasn't brave and strong. RJ reluctantly pushed his fingertips against the door in the ceiling. Surprisingly, it swung inward quite easily.

Chapter 4

"Would you look at this," RJ gasped with admiration as he poked his head up into the open space. It stretched across the entire building. "It must be an attic," RJ said as he climbed the rest of the way into the space. Joey couldn't wait any longer. He scampered right up the ladder behind RJ.

"I want to see!" he cried out. When he reached the top of the ladder he saw that RJ was already carefully walking around.

"Be careful," he warned Joey. "These floor boards are old and could be rotted."

Joey nodded and climbed carefully up into the attic. "This is amazing," Joey said with wide eyes. "Did you know this was here?"

"No," RJ replied as he shone his flashlight across a pile of old boxes. "I don't think my parents do either."

"But what is making that sound?" Joey cringed and ducked behind RJ as the thumping started again and was even louder.

"I don't know," RJ said as he stepped bravely in front of Joey. "But we're going to find out!"

As RJ began walking toward the sound, Joey stayed right behind him.

"It could be a vampire," he whispered and trembled.

"It could not be a vampire," RJ replied with a sigh of impatience.

"Why couldn't it be a vampire?" Joey asked and peeked around RJ's arm.

"Because vampires are not real," RJ pointed out and then shivered a little as he heard the thumping again. "It's coming from behind those boxes," he whispered. The boxes were even shaking a little.

"They might be real," Joey squeaked out nervously.

"Shh," RJ frowned as he stepped a little closer to the boxes. His eyes were wide and he held his breath. Thump, thump, thump, thump. The sound came faster now. Then he heard a quiet cry.

"Oh no it is a vampire!" Joey cried out and buried his face in RJ's back.

"I think it might be," RJ grimaced as he ducked down behind the boxes. "Maybe we should just leave it alone."

"But what if it comes out at night looking for us?" Joey asked, his voice shaking with fear.

"Good point," RJ said through gritted teeth. "I think we're going to need to come back with some more tools."

"What kind of tools?" Joey asked as RJ began to back away from the boxes.

"From all of the stories I've read, we'll need garlic, some wooden stakes, and you'll need to get a hat, because you know, vampires can turn into bats!" he frowned as they neared the doorway of the attic. The thumping was still loud and the boxes were still shaking.

"I think I liked it better when vampires weren't real," Joey said nervously as he began to climb down the ladder. RJ waited for him to reach the bottom of the ladder safely before he began to climb down the ladder as well. When he was half-way down he pulled the door to the attic shut behind him.

'Well, I don't think they're real," RJ explained with a sigh. "But if I were a vampire and I needed a place to hide out, I would certainly pick a hidden attic hidden inside of a wall with a hidden door. Wouldn't you?" he asked with an arched eyebrow as they walked down the hallway.

"Maybe," Joey nodded. "But I'd prefer if it weren't so dusty," he sneezed loudly.

"I'll grab some garlic from my apartment," RJ said with a nod. "While you run to yours and grab a hat, okay? We'll meet back here in a few minutes."

"Okay," Joey nodded and started to run off, then he stopped and turned back. "RJ, don't you go up there by yourself. I don't want you to be a snack for a vampire."

"Thanks," RJ grinned at his words. "It's nice to know that you care."

"Someone has to look out for you," Joey laughed and ran off down the hall.

Chapter 5

As RJ walked back toward his apartment, his mind was spinning with this new mystery. RJ knew that vampires weren't real. But he had also known that there was no hidden door in the wall of the stairwell. He had also known that the apartment building his parents managed didn't have an attic. If he could be wrong about those two things, couldn't he be wrong about the vampire too?

He shivered at the thought and pushed the door open to his apartment. As he began gathering some cloves of garlic, he heard the thumping again. Now that he knew where it was coming from, it didn't scare him as much. But he wondered if it was possible that the vampire knew what he was up to. Would he be ready for them when they went back up to the attic?

"Where am I going to find wooden stakes?" he wondered as he looked through all the drawers in the kitchen. All he found was a box of sharpened pencils.

"Well, they are wooden," he said to himself as he looked them over. He tucked the garlic and the pencils into a small black bag that he slung over his shoulder. Then he headed back out of the apartment toward the stairwell. He spotted Joey approaching from his apartment with a big floppy sunhat on his head.

"What is that?" RJ asked with a laugh.

"It's the only hat in the house!" Joey said and stuck out his tongue. "Besides, it covers all of my head!"

"I guess it'll have to do," RJ nodded and they walked toward the stairs. When they reached the stairwell with the hidden door, they both stared at the wall in amazement. There really was no way to tell that there was a door there.

Chapter 6

"I wonder if it will open again," RJ said as he pushed lightly on the wall. It didn't move an inch.

"Oh no, what if we can't get back in?" Joey gasped out.

"Why would it only open once?" RJ wondered with confusion. "What did I do differently last time?" He pushed lightly on the wall again. Then he pushed a little harder. He felt the wall give slightly.

"I'm just not pushing hard enough," he said and pushed with all of his weight against the wall. It took a moment of him pushing for the door to swing open. He almost fell in again, but managed to catch himself this time before he hit the floor.

"Yes! It opened!" Joey cried out and tried to scramble into the hidden hallway behind RJ. RJ had barely gotten to his feet when Joey tried to climb in, and he nearly lost his balance. He fell into a bunch of cobwebs.

"Ugh!" he cried out as he pulled them off of his face and hat. Joey didn't have any on his face because his big floppy hat protected him.

"Shh," Joey said to RJ. "You don't want to let the vampire know that we're coming," he rolled his eyes.

RJ gritted his teeth and tried to be patient. They crept quietly down the hallway to the wooden ladder. This time they knew what to expect as they approached. RJ climbed the ladder first and Joey held on to it as he did. When Joey started climbing up, RJ held the ladder steady for him. Then they both huddled down very quietly in the shadows of the attic.

"Do you hear it?" Joey whispered to RJ.

"I do," RJ said quietly. "But it doesn't sound as loud." In fact the thumping was more of a light tapping now. RJ wondered if the vampire had settled down and perhaps went to sleep. He wasn't sure if vampires actually slept. Either way it seemed like a good time to sneak up on him.

As they approached the stack of boxes where the sound was coming from, RJ tried to keep his footsteps soundless. He had his bag unzipped and ready. He reached in and pulled out two cloves of garlic. He gave one to Joey and held one himself.

"When we get to the boxes, toss it over," he whispered as they drew closer.

"What if he gets mad?" Joey cringed with concern.

"Even if he's mad, the garlic should slow him down," RJ tried to reassure him. But he wasn't feeling so confident about that himself. "On the count of three," he advised, his voice was barely able to be heard.

Joey closed his eyes tightly as he crouched down in front of the boxes.

"I still don't think it's a good idea to make the vampire mad," he growled through his clenched teeth.

"Maybe not," RJ said in a whisper. "But we've got to get him out of this attic somehow, don't you think?"

"Yes," Joey sighed.

"One," RJ looked directly at Joey to make sure that he was counting with him. "Two," Joey nodded and readied his clove of garlic "Three!" RJ shouted and sprung up in the air and tossed his clove of garlic over the boxes. Joey jumped up at the same time and tossed his garlic as well. Then they dropped back down behind the stack of boxes.

They were doing their best to disappear into the floor. Behind the boxes they heard a flurry of movement and thumping.

"See you made him mad," Joey hissed with annoyance.

"Shh," RJ pleaded. He covered his hat with his hands, and signaled for Joey to do the same. "Just in case he turned into a bat," he warned. They heard a lot of thumping and fluttering and even a quiet screech. "Oh it's really mad," Joey hissed as he tried to hide his face under the floppy sides of his hat. The pile of boxes was shaking so badly that the stack began to get unsteady.

"It's coming for us," Joey whimpered.

"No it's not, the garlic has to work!" Joey insisted. He reached into his black bag and pulled out the wooden pencils that he had brought with him. He handed one to Joey. "Be very careful," he warned Joey. "They're very sharp."

Joey nodded solemnly. Then there was another screech and even more thumping. "Can I have another?" Joey gulped. RJ thought about it for a moment and then nodded. He handed Joey another pencil and then tried to be as brave as he could.

"We're going to have to see what's behind there," he said quietly. "If he's not going to come to us, we're going to have to go to him."

"Do we really have to?" Joey closed his eyes briefly.

"Either that or he's going to jump over those boxes to get us," RJ explained. "I'd rather have the upper hand, wouldn't you?"

Joey nodded silently. The boxes were shaking like crazy. "I'll stand up first," RJ whispered. "If I can't get him down, then you run for the ladder. You go downstairs and get my Dad," he met Joey's eyes sternly. "I mean it. I can't have you getting eaten by a vampire."

"You can't be eaten by a vampire either," Joey pointed out.

Chapter 7

"I'll be fine," RJ insisted and then took a deep breath. He could smell the garlic he had thrown. He could only hope that it was going to work to weaken the vampire so that he would have a chance to stab him with the pencil.

In a flash of movement, he stood up from the floor and swung his arm up into the air with his pencil ready. In the same moment that he stood up, the pile of boxes was knocked over, and all of the boxes fell on top of him.

"Ah!" RJ screamed out as he was knocked backwards by the boxes. "Joey run!" he shouted to his young friend who was crawling out from under the boxes. "He's smarter than we thought! Run! As fast as you can!"

RJ cried out and tried to struggle out from underneath the boxes. They were not too heavy. In fact it almost felt as if there was very little in them. Maybe the vampire just used them to protect himself from anyone who might find the hidden attic.

Joey ran for the doorway of the attic, but he slipped on the dust that covered the wooden floorboards. He slid a few feet and then landed in a pile of floppy hat and cleats.

"Oof," he moaned as he had hit his shoulder pretty hard.

"Joey get up!" RJ shouted as he finally climbed out from under the boxes. "You've got to get out of here," he insisted as he got his balance. He turned around to face what he expected to be a vampire, with his pencil held high in the air. What he saw instead was a pile of boxes. He didn't see any vampire, or any other supernatural monster for that matter.

"He must be in his bat form!" RJ cried out with surprise. "Look out Joey! He could be anywhere!" he ducked down and began searching along the ceiling of the attic. "Where are you, you nocturnal beast?" he shouted out, trying to sound as brave as he could.

Chapter 8

Joey had managed to get to his feet but his big floppy hat had slid down on his face, making it hard for him to see. He was pulling at it as he stumbled around, trying to get it off of his face.

RJ was walking backwards with his pencil high in the air, searching for the bat. As he walked backwards, he didn't see Joey stumbling back in his direction. The two collided and both shrieked in fear. RJ spun around, ready to attack. Luckily he knew to be careful with the pencil and never strike unless he knew it was a vampire.

Joey did look pretty strange with the floppy hat on his face, but he did not look like a vampire. He lowered his pencil quickly.

"Sorry Joey, I thought you were the vampire," he gasped out. He helped Joey pull off the floppy hat.

"Where is he?" Joey asked when he could speak again, hat free.

"I don't know," RJ admitted nervously. Then they both heard the creak of the wooden ladder that led up to the hidden attic.

"Oh no," Joey gasped out. "Maybe that's him."

"Maybe he got past us," RJ cringed and looked toward the opening.

"And now he's coming back to eat us," Joey cried out with fear. He ducked behind RJ.

They watched as a shadowy figure slowly emerged from the open door of the attic. He was very tall, and looked pretty strong. He was definitely a full grown vampire.

"Run! Hide!" RJ cried out. He didn't think any amount of pencils was going to protect them from the size of that vampire. The two boys ran for cover behind the fallen pile of boxes. As they ducked down, RJ heard the thumping again, along with another screech.

"Oh no, it's right next to us," Joey whimpered as he began to slide backward on the floor.

"There must be two of them," RJ whispered as he too scooted away from the sound of the thumping.

"Who's there?" the shadowy figure shouted from the front of the attic.

"What are we going to do?" Joey cried out as he continued to scoot across the floor.

RJ was out of garlic. His pencils weren't going to work. He was sure that both he and Joey were done for.

"Whoever is up here, you're in big trouble!" the shadowy figure shouted out.

RJ froze. He knew that voice very well. That was his father's angry voice.

"Dad?" RJ stuck his head up over the pile of boxes.

"RJ?" his father called out as he walked closer to the boxes.

"Dad! Be careful!" RJ shouted out. "There's a vampire up here."

"A vampire?" his father called out. "That's ridiculous! There's no such thing as vampires!"

Chapter 9

"There is this time!" RJ said with a frown as he jumped to his feet.

"Just try to calm down boys," RJ's father said as he crept closer to them. "You've just scared yourself being up in this attic," he shone the flashlight that he was carrying in their direction. It had a much stronger beam than the ones that the boys were carrying.

The light revealed something very strange. There was something wriggling and moving around in the boxes, but it didn't look like a vampire. It didn't even look like a bat. But it did have feathers.

"Back up boys," RJ's father said as he moved closer to the creature under the boxes. "It looks like we have someone who needs a little help," he said quietly. When he pulled the boxes aside he revealed a large owl, flopping back and forth and trying to get up off of the ground.

"Wow," RJ said in a whisper as he saw the long wings of the owl. "Is he hurt or something?"

"Yes," RJ's father said. "It looks that way. Hand me one of those boxes," he murmured. "But move very slowly, we don't want to scare him more than he already is."

RJ felt bad that they had probably been the ones to scare the owl. He opened one of the boxes and found some old curtains inside. He left them in there as a cushion for the owl. "Here you go," he handed the box to his father. RJ's father gently eased the owl into the box.

"He must have gotten in here somehow," he said as he glanced around the attic. "Until you two started making all that noise, I had no idea this attic was even here. How did you find it?"

"We heard thumping," Joey said as he peeked over the side of the box at the owl.

"It must have been the owl's wings thumping against the floor," RJ suggested as he studied the owl too. The owl seemed to know he was going to be helped, because he was calm.

"Well the two of you should have told me, instead of exploring on your own," RJ's father said sternly. "But at least this little guy will get the help he needs. Let's get him downstairs and to a vet who can help him. It looks like he might have a broken wing."

"Okay," RJ nodded and helped him carry the box to the doorway of the attic.

Chapter 10

"I can understand why you two were frightened," RJ's father said. "When I heard all that noise, I was frightened too."

"I wasn't scared," RJ insisted as he held the box until his father climbed down halfway on the wooden ladder. He carefully handed it down to his father who took it the rest of the way down the ladder.

"Of course you weren't," he said as RJ climbed the rest of the way down the ladder. "You're never scared of anything," his father smiled knowingly.

"I was," Joey said with wide eyes. "I thought the owl was a vampire, and that you were a vampire!"

"Good thing I wasn't," RJ's father chuckled. "I guess that's why the attic smells like garlic, hm?" he grinned at them.

"Maybe," RJ whistled innocently.

"Well now that we know the attic is there, I'll have someone come in to make sure it's safe. I'm sure we can think of something to do with it."

"Maybe a game room?" RJ suggested hopefully.

"Oh, or a roller skating rink?" Joey asked with a grin.

"Uh, I was thinking more of storage for all of the tenants," RJ's father laughed. "But I will think about your ideas. Until then, the two of you need to make sure that you don't go up here alone. It might not be safe."

"I think we know that now," RJ said with wide eyes. He was never going to look at a wooden ladder the same way again. As they walked back down the hidden hallway, RJ leaned over to Joey.

"See, I told you there's no such thing as vampires!" he hissed.

"Well," Joey frowned. "Maybe there are vampires, they're just not your Dad!"

RJ groaned but he couldn't help but laugh at Joey's silly smile.

RJ - Boy Detective #3

Alien Goo!

PJ Ryan

RJ – Boy Detective #3:
Alien Goo!

Chapter 1

RJ and Joey were working on a project together. They were building toy boats out of Styrofoam and plastic. They were going to have races with them over the weekend. Joey added a toy pirate to his boat and drew skull and cross bone symbols on the Styrofoam. He knew that they might wash off in the water, but he didn't care.

RJ's boat was a little bigger. It had a mast and sail that he had made out of a piece of plastic bag and toothpicks. He drew his very own flag on the sail. It was a magnifying glass along with a big question mark.

As they built the boats they came up with an idea of a story between the two boats. RJ's boat would be searching for the pirate boat. Of course, he would be trying to solve the mystery of the vanishing pirate. It was a book that they had both recently read.

Since RJ loved being a detective, he always had on a detective hat. He had a large collection in many different colors. By the time they finished the boats, it was already getting late.

"I was hoping we would get to test them out tonight," RJ frowned as he glanced out the window of his apartment.

"We can still go," Joey suggested. "My Mom won't be home until late tonight and as long as we're careful, I don't think she would mind."

Joey was three years younger than RJ and RJ looked out for him after school until his Mom got home. He nodded a little. "We can make it quick," RJ said.

They grabbed their boats and hurried out of the apartment building that they both lived in. RJ's parents were the managers of the building, so he knew just about everyone who lived there. They lived very close to a city park, which had a small duck pond. It was like an oasis in the middle of the bustling city.

The sun had already set when they ran into the park. As they each tested their boats, they were treated to an unusual view. With the lights of the city being so bright, the stars were often drowned out. But, since they were in the middle of the park and the night was fairly clear, they had the chance to see some. RJ pointed them out to Joey with a smile.

"Wow, I've never seen so many in the sky," RJ said with admiration.

"Look how bright they are," Joey added with surprise. The two stared up at the sky. The harder they stared, the more it seemed as if those bright stars were moving around.

"Uh, Joey, do you see that?" RJ asked curiously.

"Yeah, I don't think stars are supposed to do that," Joey said as he scratched the top of his head.

"Maybe it's just clouds moving over them," RJ suggested. He always looked for the most logical solutions first.

"Maybe," Joey said and shivered. "But let's get out of here, okay?"

"Okay," RJ nodded. "We need to get back before your Mom gets home anyway."

They grabbed their boats and ran back toward the apartment building. As they left the park, RJ glanced over his shoulder one last time to take in the sight of the bright stars. He did find it odd that they were so very bright.

Chapter 2

The next day RJ was hurrying out of his last class for the day. It was Friday and he was looking forward to spending the weekend hanging out with Joey. They were going to have their first race at the duck pond early Saturday morning, but that didn't mean they couldn't take the boats for a spin that afternoon.

He was in such a hurry that he lost his footing on the stairs that led out of the school. He grabbed on to the railing of the steps to steady himself. When he did, his hand slid through something slippery and cold. When he pulled his hand away, the green goo that he had touched stretched from the railing to his hand.

"Ugh! Gross!" RJ complained as he shook his hand to try to get the goop off. The goop just got stringier. RJ frowned and wiped his hand across the leg of his jeans. This only smeared the goo all over and his hand was still sticky.

"Yuck," he sighed as he realized he would have to walk home like this. On the way home RJ was still fuming. He wondered what the stuff was and how it had gotten on the railing.

"It's Friday," he reminded himself. "And I'm going to have a good weekend."

When he got home he changed his clothes and washed his hands. By the time he was finished, Joey was knocking on the door. RJ answered the door, still feeling a little grossed out.

"What's wrong?" Joey asked when he noticed the scowl on RJ's face.

"Some prankster left goo on the railing at school," RJ replied with a shrug. "If I didn't know any better, I'd think it might be Mouse or Rebekah up to one of their tricks. But I know they're not in town."

"Hm, well maybe it was an accident?" Joey suggested. "Like something came off of an art project or something?"

"Maybe," RJ nodded a little. "Hey, let's get the boats down to the park before it gets too dark."

"Good idea," Joey smiled.

Chapter 3

At the park Joey and RJ had to wait for a few little kids that were skipping stones in the water. They didn't want their boats to get capsized by a pebble. So they sat down on a nearby bench.

"I wonder if the water is warm enough yet to stick our feet in?" RJ suggested.

"Let's find out!" Joey grinned.

They both tossed off their shoes and socks. Then they walked down to the edge of the water. It wasn't a swimming pond, but it was okay to dip your toes in. When RJ's toe touched the top of the water, he shivered.

"I don't think it's warm enough yet," he laughed and shook his head. But Joey was a little braver and stuck his whole foot in.

"It's not so bad," he said through chattering teeth.

"I don't believe you," RJ laughed louder. The kids that were skipping stones stopped playing, so RJ and Joey put their boats in the water.

"They look great," Joey said proudly.

"Hm, I wonder if we could add a motor to the back, or maybe some little water guns to the pirate ship?" he suggested.

"Or we could just hook them up to a duck?" Joey laughed at his own joke.

"That's actually not a bad idea," RJ said, seriously considering how they might be able to do that. It was getting dark, so the boys retrieved their boats. They walked back to the bench and began putting their shoes and socks back on.

After RJ pulled his sock on he grabbed his shoes. Without looking he shoved his foot inside one of his shoes. He felt something cold and squishy against his sock.

"What-" he started to say. When he pulled his foot out of the shoe, he gasped. "Ugh! Not again!" he huffed.

"Oh what is that?" Joey gasped as RJ pulled his foot all the way out of his shoe. His cheeks reddened when he saw the green goo stretch from inside of his shoe to the bottom of his sock.

"That is not cool," RJ sighed as he looked at his sock and his shoe. "I wonder if it will come out?" he sat down hard on the park bench and shook his head. "Someone is really trying to get me upset."

"But why the goo?" Joey wondered. "Doesn't that seem strange to you?"

"Of course it does," RJ nodded. "I can't even tell what it is. I mean, it's not quite slime, and it's not quite goo. It's something slippery and sticky at the same time."

"I've never seen anything like it," Joey frowned. Then he paused a moment before he looked up at RJ. "Do you think that maybe it had something to do with what we saw last night?"

"What do you mean?" RJ asked with confusion.

"I mean, the lights in the sky," Joey reminded him shyly. "That was pretty strange and so is this. Do you think it could be related?"

"Uh," RJ considered that for a moment. "I hadn't really thought about it I guess," he glanced up at the sky. "I mean how could they be?" then suddenly he looked back at Joey. "You're talking about aliens aren't you?" he asked suspiciously.

"Maybe," Joey murmured as he rocked back on the heels of his shoes. "I mean, don't you think it's possible that they saw us? Maybe they're targeting us?"

"Why would they do that?" RJ asked, and then shook his head sharply. "I mean, it's not possible. It can't be aliens," he said firmly.

"Alright, but that doesn't look like it comes from anywhere on earth," Joey pointed to the goo again. RJ sighed and took off his sock. He tucked it into his goo-filled shoe. Then he and Joey began to walk back toward the apartment building.

"I don't know where this goo came from, but I'm sure it couldn't be alien made," RJ said calmly. "I mean, what would aliens want with us?"

"I don't know," Joey shrugged a little. "Maybe they need a detective, like you," Joey grinned.

"Hm," RJ considered that. "Well I am a good detective, but I'm sure they could find another one on their own planet."

"Maybe they're aliens that don't know how to be detectives," Joey pointed out. "Maybe they want to take you back to their planet so that you can teach them how to be detectives."

"Haha," RJ smirked at his friend. "I know you're just trying to scare me."

"Is it working?" Joey asked with a gleam in his eyes.

"No," RJ said firmly. "I don't know why there is goo everywhere I go yet, but I will find out. Like you said, I am a great detective."

"Did I say that?" Joey asked and then ran ahead of RJ before he could catch him. RJ hobbled after him, trying his best to hop on one foot.

Chapter 4

RJ was awake in his bed that night. He was trying to figure out where the goo was coming from. Even though he suspected that Joey had been joking about the aliens, the more he thought about it, the more possible it seemed.

They had been the only ones by the pond. So if the aliens had been looking down, they would have only seen them. So maybe they decided they wanted to do something to frighten them. Or maybe the green goo was being used in some way to try to take over RJ's mind. He shivered at the thought.

Aliens had much more advanced technology than humans. If they were real, of course. So maybe the goo was meant to do something to RJ. What if he woke up in the middle of the night without even knowing it and walked out to some alien spaceship? Would he be whisked away before he even knew what was happening?

The more RJ thought about it, the more frightened he became. By the time the sun rose, he was determined to find out who was behind the goo. Joey called him first thing.

"Are we still having our race?" he asked hopefully. "Or did the aliens goo you?"

"No, the aliens didn't goo me," RJ replied with annoyance. "But I do think we need to be more careful about that stuff."

"Me too," Joey agreed. "I had a scary dream about aliens made out of green goo. What if they're leaving it behind?"

RJ sighed. "Just calm down Joey, I really don't think it could be aliens."

"Alright," Joey replied. "I'll be over in ten minutes."

"I'll have the boats ready," RJ promised.

When Joey showed up at RJ's apartment he knocked on the door.

"Come in!" RJ called out as he picked up the boats.

Joey reached for the doorknob. RJ heard a loud shriek from outside the door. He ran to the door, hoping that Joey wasn't hurt.

"What's wrong? What happened?" RJ asked as he opened the door. Joey held up his trembling hand. It was covered in green goo. So was the door knob.

"Alright, that's it," RJ said sharply as he tugged Joey inside. He marched into the kitchen and grabbed some paper towels to clean off the door knob. Joey washed his hand off in the sink, still shaking a little. It was funny to him when RJ got the goo on him, but not so funny when he got it on himself.

"No alien is going to ruin our weekend!" RJ said sternly. "We're going to find out just who is doing this. Alien or human, they are going to have some explaining to do."

"Yeah!" Joey said sternly. Then he frowned. "RJ how do you think we're going to make an alien explain itself?"

"I'm hoping it's not an alien," RJ shuddered. "I'm sorry Joey but we're going to have to put off our race until tomorrow. Today we are alien hunting, or goo hunting at least."

"Let's do it," Joey agreed, but he didn't sound as brave as usual. "What's the plan?" he asked nervously.

"Well, it seems to me that the aliens are doing things when we're not looking," RJ said calmly. "I wasn't looking at school before I touched the railing. I also didn't look at my shoe while we were at the park. Now, you didn't look at the door handle before you touched it. So, they must be waiting until we're not around to do these things.

I say, let's leave our shoes outside in the hall. Then we can hide out and see if the alien takes the bait and fills them up with goo."

"That's a good idea," Joey nodded. "I think."

"What do you mean you think?" RJ asked with surprise.

"Well, I just don't know if it's a good idea to hunt an alien," Joey pointed out. "If we do catch it, then what are we going to do with it?" Joey asked.

"We'll figure that out after we catch it," RJ said with a sigh. He didn't want to believe it was an alien, but if it was, Joey did have a point. He had no idea how to trap an alien.

Chapter 5

The two boys put their shoes out into the hallway. Then RJ climbed into one of the empty trash cans. He knew it would be empty as Mrs. Culpepper always emptied them every Saturday morning for the weekend. He fit just right inside of it.

Joey ducked down behind one of the fake bushes that made the hallway look more like a jungle than an apartment building hallway.

"I think we're going to be here a while," Joey sighed as there was no one coming in either direction.

"Maybe," RJ frowned. It was not the way he had hoped to spend his Saturday. Not long after, RJ heard the elevator doors sliding open.

"Shh," he told Joey, just in case he hadn't noticed. Then he held his breath as he heard footsteps slowly approaching.

Didn't aliens glide? He was pretty sure they did. Joey peered through the leaves on the bush. RJ peeked out of the flap out of the trash can. What they saw was not what they expected. It was RJ's mother heading for the apartment. She had gone out for groceries but had returned without any.

RJ stayed quiet as he knew if she discovered that he was hiding inside of the trash can, no amount of explaining would keep him from being grounded. When she reached for the door handle she gasped. RJ winced as he realized he must have missed some of the goo.

"RJ," she growled. RJ winced again, as he was sure he was going to get a stern talking to about washing his hands. She sighed and opened the door. A few minutes later she came back out with what had been missing. Her shopping list. Then she headed straight to the elevator.

RJ relaxed a little. He was glad that she hadn't caught him inside the trash can, but he was still waiting for the alien to show himself.

"Ugh, this is so boring," Joey complained from the other side of the hall. "What if the aliens decided to return to their planet?"

"We're staying," RJ said firmly. "At least for another hour. We have to make sure that the alien has the chance to see the shoes."

"Alright," Joey sighed and ducked down behind the bush again. A few minutes later RJ heard the elevator again. He hoped that it wouldn't be his mother and that she wouldn't notice his and Joey's shoes sitting outside of the door.

Chapter 6

RJ peeked through the flap of the trash can. What he saw at first was very surprising. All he saw was a green glow. Then beyond the glow he could see a figure. It was impossible to tell what the figure looked like, as he wore a hat with the brim pulled down over his face.

RJ was fairly certain an alien wouldn't wear a hat, but he was also fairly certain that a person wouldn't be glowing green. The figure walked slowly and quietly toward RJ's apartment. RJ sunk down in the trash can, but continued to watch.

He could see the leaves on the bush that Joey was hiding behind, beginning to move. Joey was probably very scared. He had been right. RJ had no idea what to do now that he had seen the alien. He could only watch as the alien crouched down in front of their shoes.

With his back to them, RJ couldn't see the alien put the green goo inside of his shoes, but he knew that the alien did it. When the alien stood up, he could see the goo spilling over the top of his shoe.

"Ew," RJ whispered to himself. He had just gotten his shoe clean too. He expected the alien would leave after that. But the alien was not satisfied. He walked up to the door of the apartment. Then he smeared the green goo all over the door handle again.

RJ was livid. He knew if his mother saw that, she would ground him for a week. She was not a fan of goo of any kind, especially not on door knobs.

When the alien pulled its hand away from the door knob, RJ could see the green goo dripping from his fingers. Maybe Joey had been right. Maybe the alien was made entirely of green goo!

Again RJ expected the alien to walk away. But the alien still wasn't done. It pressed its hand against the wall beside the door. When it pulled its hand away, gooey green strings stretched from its hand to the wall.

RJ was horrified. He knew that he was going to be blamed for all of this. The alien then started to turn and walk away. But RJ was too angry to let that happen. He decided he was going to make the alien clean up its mess.

"Hey!" he shouted from inside of the trash can. "You can't do that!" he shouted again. "This is the planet Earth. And on Earth people have manners!" he sputtered out. He wasn't making much sense, but he didn't care.

Across from him Joey ducked out from behind the bush. But his leg got caught on the pot and he fell forward right into the path of the alien.

"Joey!" RJ squealed. He tried to climb out of the trash can, but he was more stuck then he thought. When he tried to wriggle his way free, he rocked the trash can. Instead of being able to climb out, the entire trash can tipped over, right between Joey and the alien.

As RJ made his way out of the trash can, Joey struggled to get to his feet. The alien looked at both of them. Then it sprinted down the hall away from the elevator. RJ knew that there was another elevator on the other side of the hall. There was also a doorway that led to the stairs.

"Wait!" he shouted as he tried to get to his feet. "Get back here you alien!" RJ shouted even louder. He shouted so loud that some of his neighbors opened their doors to peek out into the hallway. When they saw the overturned trash can and the dripping goo, they closed their doors again.

RJ frowned as he helped Joey to his feet. He was about to chase after the alien when he remembered that he didn't have any shoes on. And, he couldn't put any on, because they were filled with green goo.

Chapter 7

"Oh that alien," he growled.

"He was scary!" Joey said as he looked down the hall. "Where do you think he went?"

"I don't know," RJ said, still quite angry. "But I'm going to find him. And when I do, he's going clean all of this up. Because I'm not getting grounded just because an alien decided to goo my shoes."

"Speaking of shoes," Joey said as he looked at the shoes outside of the door. "I guess we didn't really think that through."

"Actually," RJ said with a snap of his fingers. "I did," he walked over to their shoes and showed Joey how he had lined the inside of them with saran wrap. They still had to get rid of the goo, but at least their shoes wouldn't have to be cleaned out.

"You are just so clever," Joey said with a shake of his head.

"Why thank you," RJ replied as he reached for the door knob on the door of the apartment. "I like to think that I'm a little smarter than an alien," he explained.

"Uh," Joey started to speak, but before he could, it was too late. RJ had grabbed the doorknob covered in green goo.

"Ugh," RJ complained as he pulled his hand back from the doorknob and whined. "This is ridiculous. I can't believe I fell for it again."

"Well, I guess it must be pretty hard to be smarter than an alien," Joey pointed out, hoping to make his friend feel better.

"I guess," RJ sighed again as he pushed open the door. Once they had cleaned RJ's hand, their shoes and the doorknob, they headed back out into the hall.

"So what are we going to do now?" Joey asked. "We can't just let an alien run around spreading goo everywhere."

"No, I guess we can't," RJ replied with a huff. "But how can we find him now? It's too late. He's been gone for quite some time."

"That's true," Joey agreed. "I guess we'll just have to hide out in the hallway again."

"No," RJ shook his head slightly. "I don't want to do that again. We don't know anything about this alien. He, or it, could be very dangerous. We don't want to be sitting right in front of it, saying hey, come and get me alien!"

"Good point," Joey agreed with a chuckle.

"Look," RJ pointed to something he saw on the floor.

"What is it?" Joey asked and crouched down to take a closer look.

"I think it's a clue," RJ said with a smirk. "It looks like a spot of goo."

"Yes it does," Joey agreed with a grin.

"Maybe he dripped all the way home," RJ said hopefully. "Let's follow the spots and find out."

Chapter 8

They followed the spots to the end of the hallway. They led to the door that led to the stairs. They followed the spots down the stairs. There was green goo on the railing. But this time RJ was careful not to touch it.

"Watch your step," he warned Joey. "This stuff is slippery."

Joey nodded and they continued to the bottom of the steps. There was a door at the bottom of the steps that led to the lobby, and another door that led to the outside of the apartment building. The spots went to the door that led to the outside of the apartment building.

"Oh no," Joey sighed. "We're never going to find him now. I bet he stepped outside and then his spaceship beamed him right up."

"Maybe," RJ said thoughtfully. "But maybe not. Let's see where the spots lead."

He opened up the door and saw that the spots continued out on to the sidewalk.

"See, not beamed up yet," RJ said cheerfully. In fact, the spots led to the crosswalk. The street was busy with traffic. So they had to wait for the walk sign.

"He must have crossed the street," RJ said. "Because the spots go right to the edge of the sidewalk."

"Yes," Joey nodded. "But with all those cars driving back and forth, there won't be anything on the road to see."

"No, just a lot of cars with goo on their tires," RJ pointed out with a grin.

"So how are we going to find the alien now?" Joey asked with concern.

"Just follow me," RJ said calmly. The walk sign came on and together the boys walked carefully across the street. When they reached the other side, RJ pointed to the sidewalk. "See?" he said with a smile. "The spots start again."

"Perfect!" Joey exclaimed. They began to follow the spots down the sidewalk. They didn't have to walk far because the spots led right to the door of the apartment building across from theirs.

"So the alien lives here?" Joey asked with confusion. "I didn't think that an alien would live in an apartment."

"Neither did I," RJ replied as he held open the door for Joey to step inside. Once they were inside there were spots that led along the carpet of the lobby. They led right up to a maid who was scrubbing the carpet clean.

"Oh no," RJ sighed. "She must be cleaning up the spots. Which means we've reach a dead end," he sighed.

"Maybe not!" Joey exclaimed as he pointed to the elevator button. It had a green glob on it.

"Good eye Joey," RJ smiled. "We'll hunt down this alien yet."

As they rode up in the elevator they could tell which floor the alien got off on, because there was another green glob.

"This is one messy alien," Joey said with a shake of his head. But he was starting to look a little scared. "What are we going to do if we find him?" he wondered.

"We'll just have to see what we're dealing with first," RJ said.

They didn't have long to consider it, because as they stepped off of the elevator, a glowing figure was about to step on.

Chapter 9

"You!" RJ exclaimed.

"Uh-" the alien said, his eyes wide. He looked more like a boy about RJ's age than an alien. But he was still glowing.

"Are you an alien?" Joey asked fearfully as the elevator doors closed behind them. RJ's heart was racing as they were trapped between the alien and the elevator. Instead of answering, the alien began to run. He ran as fast as he could down the hall. RJ and Joey began to chase after him. The alien was half way down the hall when he slipped in a pile of his own goo. He landed hard on his knee and immediately began wailing.

"My knee, my knee," he cried. "I scraped my knee!"

RJ slowed to a stop as he studied the alien. Did aliens cry? Did aliens even have knees? This one sure seemed to, as there was a little blood soaking through his pants.

"Uh, are you okay?" RJ asked hesitantly. He wasn't sure if he should be nice, but he hated to see anyone get hurt.

"Yes," the alien said, and sniffled. He was hiding his face behind his knee.

"You're not an alien, are you?" RJ asked suspiciously as he tried to get a closer look at the boy.

"No," the alien sighed. "I'm not an alien," he admitted. "My name's Nathan."

"Nathan?" Joey asked and then shook his head. "That's definitely not an alien name."

"Why did you do this?" RJ demanded with annoyance. "Do you know how much trouble you've caused?"

"I didn't mean to cause any trouble," Nathan replied, still hiding his face. "I'm sorry. I felt bad after what happened and I was coming back to tell you the truth. I didn't want you to be angry with me."

RJ shook his head. "But why did you do it in the first place?"

Nathan sighed and finally peeked out from behind his knee. "I just moved here," he explained quietly. "I've seen you at school, and I've heard all these stories about how you're a great detective. I wanted to be friends."

"Funny way of showing it," Joey muttered, but RJ elbowed him lightly in the side.

"You were too shy to say hello?" RJ asked. He could understand that. Until he began doing detective work he was always very shy also.

"Yeah," Nathan nodded. "I know it seems strange, but I thought if I created a mystery for you to solve, that maybe you would want to be friends."

"Well," RJ crossed his arms. "I didn't like the mystery. I mean it was clever, but oh so very messy, and I'm pretty sure that my Mom is going to think I've been bathing in jello."

Nathan couldn't help but laugh at that. "I'm really sorry. I understand if you never want to talk to me again."

"Hey, I said I didn't like the mystery. I didn't say I didn't like you," RJ pointed out. "Let's get your knee cleaned up and then we can get the rest of the goo cleaned up. Sound good?"

"Sure," Nathan sighed with relief. As RJ and Joey helped Nathan toward his apartment, RJ's mind was already on boats.

"So Nathan, how are you with ducks?"

Mystery Poo!

PJ Ryan

RJ – Boy Detective #4:

Mystery Poo!

Chapter 1

RJ was setting up his newest video game in the living room. He knew that Joey would be home from school in a few minutes, and he couldn't wait to show it to him.

RJ looked out for Joey in the afternoons since his mother worked until dinner. Although at first RJ had seen Joey as just a kid to babysit, he soon became good friends with him. He always had some clever ideas and he was helpful when RJ had a mystery to solve.

RJ adjusted the black and white checked detective's hat that he had chosen to wear. He had a large collection of them and he always wore a different one, depending on how he felt that day.

RJ was feeling determined, determined to beat the new video game in one afternoon. He and Joey had been coming up with strategies for about a week in an attempt to beat the game, but the game had just been delivered that day, so neither of them had actually played it.

RJ was very interested in it because it dealt with knights and dragons, which were some of his favorite subjects, aside from detective work.

When he heard a knock on the door of his apartment he knew that Joey had arrived. RJ hurried to open the door for Joey and then ran right back to the video game to connect the last wires to the television.

He heard the door close behind him, and Joey's footsteps through the front hall, which was tile. But before he could actually see Joey, he smelled him. RJ's eyes widened at the scent. It was a horrible smell. It was a disgusting smell. It was-

"Ugh, I think I stepped in something," Joey muttered as he lifted up his shoe and looked at the bottom of it.

"Gross!" RJ scowled as he saw the caked dog poop on the bottom of Joey's shoe. Of course he had walked on it for some time, causing the dog poop to get wedged into the crevices and cracks of the sole of his shoe. "Get that shoe out of here!" RJ demanded and pinched his nose closed to block out the smell.

"Okay, okay," Joey sighed and started to walk back toward the door.

"No!" RJ gasped. "Don't walk on the floor. You're tracking it all over!" he complained.

"Sorry," Joey sighed and began hopping on one foot toward the door. As he did he knocked off little globs of the dog poop on to the floor.

"No!" RJ cried out again. "Just take it off! Before you get even more poop everywhere!"

Joey sighed and unlaced his shoe. He took the shoe off and looked up at RJ with a frown. "I'm sorry."

"It's okay, it's not like you meant to step in dog poop," RJ pointed out. "It's just we can't let it get everywhere," then suddenly his mouth dropped open. "Oh no you didn't ride up in the elevator did you?" he asked.

RJ and Joey lived in a tall apartment building that RJ's parents managed.

"Sure I did," Joey shrugged a little. Then he winced. "Oh no, that's not good," he realized. RJ hurried into the kitchen and grabbed a plastic grocery bag. He handed it to Joey with his nose still pinched. When he spoke, his pinched nose made his voice sound very funny.

"Just put it in there," RJ insisted. Then he ran back to the kitchen for a roll of paper towels. He sighed as he cleaned up the smudges and clumps that Joey had left on the floor.

"Let's get this downstairs and clean it off," RJ said with a shake of his head. "I don't want to clean it in here."

"Okay," Joey nodded and held the bag out in front of him as far as he could stretch it.

Chapter 2

As they walked down the hall, RJ in his boots, and Joey in one shoe and one sock, they saw a group of people getting off the elevator. Actually, they were really running off the elevator. They couldn't get out of there fast enough.

"Ugh, what a terrible smell!" one of the women cried out.

"It wasn't me!" the man with them insisted. "I promise it wasn't!" he pleaded as the women hurried away from him. One turned her head and glowered at the man. "It wasn't!" he insisted, but the women did not seem to believe him. The man huffed and hung his head as he walked down the hall. RJ stuck his nose in the elevator and immediately regretted it. He ducked back out and cringed.

"We've definitely got a poopy situation," he sighed and shook his head. The carpet inside the elevator was smeared with the offending substance.

"Oh Mrs. Weathers is not going to be happy about this," RJ muttered as he pinched his nose.

"I'm going to be in so much trouble," Joey moaned, still holding the plastic bag out in front of him as far as he could.

"You shouldn't be," RJ growled with annoyance. "This is the city and there are rules here about letting your dogs go potty all over the place!" he still sounded very strange as he was still pinching his nose shut.

"You can't just let your dog poo where people walk! Then everyone steps in poo! This is what happens!" he was still complaining about this as he stepped off of the elevator. When the doors opened Mrs. Weathers was standing right outside.

"Ah!" she cried out when the scent hit her. "Oh what have you two boys done in there?" she demanded crossly. Mrs. Weathers was the head maid of the hotel and the smelly situation had obviously been reported to her.

"It wasn't Joey's fault!" RJ came quickly to his younger friend's defense. "Someone didn't clean up after their dog. Poor Joey has poo all over his shoe!"

"Ugh," Mrs. Weathers shook her head and pinched her nose as she pointed to the plastic bag that Joey was holding.

"Is that the shoe with the poo?" she asked nervously.

"It is," Joey said sadly. "I was going to clean it off outside."

"You do that," Mrs. Weathers huffed, or tried to. With her nose pinched, it came out a bit more like a cough. "And don't bring your shoe back in here until you know that it is clean, understand?" she said sternly.

"Yes Ma'am," Joey said with a sigh as he stepped all the way off of the elevator. There was nothing that Joey could do to hide the scent as he carried the shoe through the apartment building's lobby. He got a lot of annoyed looks from the adults that were milling about, checking their mail or stopping to talk to one another. Joey hung his head, but RJ walked tall beside him.

"Don't worry Joey. We're going to make sure this never happens again," RJ said firmly.

Chapter 3

When they stepped outside RJ began searching the sidewalk for the pile of poo. He knew it couldn't be far, as Joey only walked a block to the apartment building from his bus stop.

"Do you know where you stepped on it?" RJ asked curiously as he continued to search the sidewalk.

"Over there," Joey pointed to the squashed pile of poo.

"Look at that," RJ said with a shake of his head. "It's right in the middle of the sidewalk. How could anyone miss it?" he growled. "And look!" he added with frustration, as he pointed to the sign above the pile. The sign was very clear in its message.

"Please clean up after your pet" and there were small plastic baggies to use to clean up any messes that a dog might leave behind. There was even a place where the used plastic bags could be thrown away.

"There is no excuse for this," RJ said with anger in his voice. "Our whole afternoon should not be ruined by stinky dog poo because someone doesn't bother to clean up after their pet properly."

"RJ, just calm down," Joey said with a frown as he found a stick to pry the poo out of the cracks of his shoe. "There is nothing that we can do about it now. It was probably just a mistake," he added.

"With that smell?" RJ asked with a shake of his head. "I don't think anyone could overlook that. Do you?"

"I doubt it," Joey agreed with a slight shrug. "But we still have to clean it up."

"Yes, you're right," RJ frowned as he snatched a plastic bag. "We don't want anyone else stepping in this."

As he cleaned up the poo he was grumbling under his breath. "But this better never happen again."

Once they had cleaned Joey's shoe and the mess that had been left on the sidewalk. They headed back into the lobby where the smell had been mostly cleared out.

Mrs. Weathers was using the steam cleaner on a few spots on the carpet in the main lobby.

"Joey, I'm sorry if I was upset with you before," she said quickly. "I know that it wasn't your fault that you stepped in something. But is your shoe clean now?" she asked suspiciously.

"All clean Mrs. Weathers," he promised as he lifted up his shoe to show her how clean it was on the bottom.

"There's nothing in the elevator anymore, so you two are safe to go up," she promised.

"Thanks Mrs. Weathers," RJ said with a frown. "And I cleaned up the mess outside so that no one else will track it in."

"That was very thoughtful out of you RJ," Mrs. Weathers said with a sigh of relief. As RJ and Joey rode the elevator back up to RJ's apartment, RJ was still grumbling.

Chapter 4

The next day RJ decided to pick Joey up from the bus stop. He wanted to make sure that Joey didn't track anything else into the hotel, but he was also curious to see if he might catch the dog owner who had not cleaned up after his pet.

As he walked toward the bus stop he kept his eyes on the sidewalk, searching for any stinky piles. However, he didn't see anything except for a few pigeon splatters and a squirrel who seemed to be following him.

RJ had just reached the bus stop. He spotted the bus coming down the street. It was held up a little by traffic. He stepped to the edge of the sidewalk and smiled. But his smile faded as he felt his shoe squish down into something. Then he smelled the awful scent wafting up beneath his nostrils.

"No!" he shouted as he looked down at the sidewalk. He had stepped right into a pile of poo. The bus pulled up just as he was scraping the sole of his shoe against the edge of the sidewalk.

"EW!" several of the kids on the bus shouted as they spotted what RJ was doing through the windows. Joey stepped off the bus and immediately covered his nose with his hand.

"Ugh," he muttered as the bus pulled away. "Gross! Now my bus stop is going to smell!"

RJ groaned as he hadn't thought of that. He didn't want Joey to have to smell that every time he waited for the bus.

"I'm sorry Joey," RJ sighed. "I didn't mean to cause that problem. I bet we can get something to spray it off with."

"Don't worry boys, the street cleaner will take care of that," the bus driver promised just before he closed the doors.

"I can't believe that this happened again," RJ was fuming as he adjusted his hat on his head and scowled. "That's twice in a row. I'm starting to think we have a serial pooper, don't you?" he glanced over at Joey who had pinched his nose completely closed. He was gulping in air through his mouth, so he could only nod in return.

As they walked toward the apartment building, RJ was so busy getting angry that he didn't even notice the big pile of poop right in front of them. Luckily, Joey did.

"Watch out RJ!" Joey shouted as he gave his older friend a slight shove. That shove was just enough to keep RJ's foot from stepping down into the pile of poo.

"Ugh!" he cried out. "That's it! No more! I will find out exactly who is doing this. It is not that much to ask. Just clean up the poop!"

"Well if Detective RJ is on the case, then I know that we will figure it out," Joey said with confidence. "But first can we finish playing that new game?" he asked hopefully.

"Of course we can," RJ agreed with a nod. "Right after I clean off my shoe," he sighed.

Chapter 5

RJ woke up very early the next morning. He had set three alarms to make sure that he got up in time. He was determined to find out who was leaving behind piles of poo on the sidewalk.

He still felt like a zombie as he stepped off of the elevator. He drifted past the doorman with a brief nod and out on to the sidewalk.

It was still dark outside. He positioned himself beside the mailbox to wait for the culprit to show up. As he waited, he thought of exactly what he was going to say to the person.

He was going to point out every sign that instructed people to clean up after their pet. He was going to ask what in the world they were feeding that poor dog. He was also going to demand that he pay a fine.

As he ran through all of these things in his mind, there was one thing he never considered. That was what he would do if the person didn't show up with their pet.

As an hour ticked by RJ remained in the same position. But his legs began to hurt. He was getting very bored of sitting in the same place.

Then RJ considered something else. Maybe whoever had done this was watching him. He looked up at the apartment building to all of the windows that looked down at him. He was pretty sure that anyone in those rooms could see him. Maybe the person didn't want to walk their dog while he was watching, because they knew that they had done something wrong.

Of course RJ felt silly for not thinking of that. He decided he would have to trick the person. He stood up, stretched out and sighed as if he had given up. Then he began walking back toward the apartment building. He tucked his hands into his pockets as if he was just going for a stroll. Then he ducked into the apartment building.

He waited until someone was walking back out. Then he walked back out with that person and ducked behind the bushes that lined the outside of the apartment building. It was a bad choice, he realized, the moment that the ants began creeping up along his boots.

"Oh no," he whispered. "Shoo!" he brushed them off of his boots, but more began to tromp right up along his boots. He was not looking forward to the chance of them getting inside the legs of his pants. When he felt a tickle on his shin, he squeaked and stood up from the bushes.

He had been so busy worrying about the ants that he hadn't even noticed there was someone walking down the sidewalk. He didn't see the dog, sniffing the sidewalk right beside the bushes.

In fact, he didn't realize what was happening as he began dancing around, trying to get the ants out of his pants, until his shoe landed in a fresh, warm pile of stinky poo.

Chapter 6

"NO!" he screamed out as he recognized the squish.

"Oh dear," he heard a shrill voice gasp out. "Oh my!" the voice cried. RJ looked up to see a woman who was barely taller than him leaning heavily on a cane. Her hair was in tight gray curls and her eyes were nearly hidden by thick round glasses. He could see them well enough to know that she was glaring at him.

"Why you just gave me such a fright," the woman huffed. "What do you think you're doing, going about, shouting at old women?" she demanded.

"I'm sorry," RJ said quickly while he was trying to scrape off his shoe at the same time. "I didn't mean to scare you," he insisted.

"Ugh," the woman reached up and pinched her nose. "Well you might be polite, but you are one smelly boy," she said with a huff. "You are a boy aren't you?" she asked. "It's hard to tell with that hat on your head."

"Yes I'm a boy," RJ replied with a frown. "And I'm not smelly-"

"Oh sonny, you are in dire need of a bath," the woman said with a shake of her head. "I mean, I know boys like to play in the dirt, but honey," she lowered her voice as if she was trying to be kind to RJ. "You smell like you've been playing in something else."

"It's not me!" RJ insisted, though he tried to be as respectful as he could. "I just stepped in this pile of dog poo!"

"Dog poo?" the woman shrieked. "Where?"

'Right here," RJ pointed to the pile, and to the bottom of his shoe. The woman squinted and leaned a little closer. Then she shook her head.

"Some people shouldn't have pets," she huffed. Then she began walking off, with her tiny white dog walking in front of her.

RJ was very confused. He was sure it was that little dog that had left the mess that he stepped in, but the woman had acted as if she had no idea who would do such a thing.

As RJ watched her walk away he reached up and took off his detective hat. He scratched his head and then sighed. He had to go clean his shoe yet again.

Chapter 7

When Joey showed up later that afternoon he found RJ glaring out the window.

"What are you doing?" Joey asked with surprise. "I thought you'd be at that video game again."

"Video games aren't real," RJ pointed out. "Piles of poo are and we're going to find out exactly how they are being left behind and by whom."

"Well I'm pretty sure we already know how," Joey giggled. RJ rolled his eyes and growled.

"This is serious Joey. Okay, I'm upset that I stepped in it and that you stepped in it, but that's not why I'm doing this. Think about what would happen if every dog owner left their pet's mess behind. We wouldn't even be walk on the sidewalk!"

"That would be pretty gross," Joey admitted and winced. "So what's the plan?"

"Well I figured if I stay here by this window long enough, I should be able to spot the dog and its owner," RJ explained.

"Well that's not much of a plan," Joey frowned. "You'll be stuck here all day."

"Hm," RJ considered Joey's words. He hadn't exactly decided what he was going to do if he got hungry or needed to use the bathroom. "Maybe you're right," he said quietly. "Instead of waiting for the dog, I need to go to the dog," he smiled and snapped his fingers. "You're brilliant Joey!"

"I am?" Joey asked with surprise and then smiled. "Okay, I am," he grinned.

"There's only one place that we can find just about all the dogs in the neighborhood," RJ explained. "At the dog park!"

"Sure, that's what I meant," Joey nodded quickly.

"Let's go," RJ grabbed his detective hat and pulled it down over his head. "It's time to crack the case," he said sternly.

Chapter 8

The dog park was not hard to find, as there was a good bit of yelping and barking coming from the area. When RJ and Joey reached it they discovered that there were a lot more dogs in their neighborhood than they thought.

"That has to be about twenty dogs," Joey gasped as he watched them running around the grass chasing each other or toys that their owners were throwing. "How are we ever going to figure out which one we're looking for?" RJ asked with concern.

"Well, I think it's more important that we figure out how we're going to escape," Joey said quickly.

"How we're going to escape?" RJ asked with confusion as he glanced over at Joey. Joey's eyes were wide as he pointed in front of him.

"Run!" he shouted. A huge dog was barreling toward both of them. Just as Joey was about to turn and flee, RJ grabbed his arm firmly.

"It's okay," he said. "He just wants to play."

He held out his hand to the dog, and let the dog sniff it. RJ smiled at the tickle of the dog's nose.

"That's a good boy," he said softly. "You just want to play huh?" RJ smiled. The big dog looked up at RJ with happy eyes and a wagging tongue. "See Joey, he's nothing to be afraid of- oof!"

RJ was knocked flat on his back in the middle of his sentence. He landed on the grass and gasped as the big dog stared down at him. RJ was scared for a moment before the big dog began licking his cheeks and nose.

"Bowser!" a man's voice called out. "Bowser get off of that boy!" he demanded as he ran up to RJ and Joey. "I'm so sorry, I usually keep him on his leash, but he got away from me," the man sighed. "You're not hurt are you?" he asked with concern.

"No I'm okay," RJ promised as the man guided Bowser off of RJ. Just as the man was about to apologize again, Bowser broke free and went running across the park. RJ started to sit up, but when he turned his head to the side he was greeted by something vile.

"Ah!" he shrieked and jumped to his feet. There was a pile of dog poo right next to where he had landed.

"Ugh, an inch to the right and you would have had that in your hair!" Joey screeched and pinched his nose tightly.

RJ looked at all the signs posted around the dog park that insisted people should clean up their dog's poo. He was even more angry than he had been when it was on the sidewalk.

"Whoever is letting their dog poo everywhere certainly seems to be doing it on purpose," RJ growled with annoyance. When RJ looked around he noticed that same little white dog and the woman who was walking him.

"I bet it was her!" he said with a huff.

"Who?" Joey asked.

"Her," RJ replied and pointed in the woman's direction.

"That's Mrs. Monahoo," Joey explained as he watched the woman walking her dog. "And that's Paulie. Paulie is always with Mrs. Monahoo."

"Well, I think she's the one leaving the messes behind," RJ muttered as he crossed his arms over his chest. "This morning, I stepped right in it."

"Hm," Joey shook his head slightly. "I don't think that's right. Mrs. Monahoo is very nice and she's lived on this block for a very long time. I'm sure she knows the rules about cleaning up after her pet."

"Well, we'll just see about that," RJ muttered. He was always respectful of his elders, but in this case he was going to have to make an exception.

Chapter 9

RJ was determined to officially catch Paulie in the act. So he followed Mrs. Monahoo home. Then he waited for her to take the dog for another walk.

When RJ heard the door open, he ducked behind a nearby building. After hiding there for a few minutes, he peeked back out. No Mrs. Monahoo. No Paulie. RJ was confused, and hid again. A few minutes later he heard footsteps.

"Aha!" RJ exclaimed as he rounded the corner of the building. He could hear the yapping of the dog and that horrible smell that wafted in the breeze. He knew that the person that had not been cleaning up after their dog was right there before him. He was more careful this time, to make sure that he didn't step in a fresh pile.

"You again!" Mrs. Monahoo gasped and glared at RJ. "I thought last time might be a mistake, but this is just downright rude!"

"Mrs. Monahoo, I didn't mean to frighten you," RJ said quickly. Then he saw it. The pile of poo, right out in the open in the middle of the sidewalk.

"That's what you said last time," Mrs. Monahoo shook her head. Then she sniffed the air and shuddered. "And you still have not taken a bath? How can you stand that smell?" she asked as she glared at him through her thick glasses.

"Excuse me Ma'am, but that smell is not coming from me," RJ said firmly. "At least not this time," he added. "It's coming from the pile of poo that your dog has just left behind."

"What?" Mrs. Monahoo growled. "I would never leave my dog's mess behind. It is every dog owner's responsibility to clean up after them! How dare you accuse me of something so terrible?" she demanded.

"Please, Mrs. Monahoo," RJ tried to speak respectfully. "How can you tell me that your dog was not the one to do it, when your dog is the only one here?"

"Impossible!" Mrs. Monahoo huffed. "In fact, I think I need to talk to your parents. Who are they?" RJ's eyes widened as he looked at Mrs. Monahoo. He knew that if his parents thought he was jumping out and scaring people, they would have a big problem with that. Would they believe him?

"But look," he pointed to the poo on the sidewalk. "It's right there," he insisted.

"I don't see anything," Mrs. Monahoo hissed. "One more time young man and I promise I will not only speak to your parents, I will speak to the police!"

Chapter 10

As she turned away from him, Joey came running up behind him.

"Did you catch her?" he asked curiously. "Did you leave the dog poo behind?"

"Yes," RJ nodded a little, but he didn't feel happy about it. In fact he felt a little sad.

"Well why don't you ask her to clean it up?" Joey asked with confusion.

"You know what Joey," RJ said thoughtfully as he watched Mrs. Monahoo toddle away.

"What?" Joey asked.

"I don't think Mrs. Monahoo is lying when she says it's not her, I think she believes it." RJ frowned. "I think that she's having a hard time seeing the poo that gets left behind."

Joey thought about that for a moment. "I guess that's possible," he said quietly.

"So she doesn't think it's her dog that's left it behind. And think about it, even if she did think that it was, how could she clean it up, if she can't see it?" he sighed and shook his head. "And to think I've been judging her for not cleaning up after her dog, when I should have been thinking about how I could help."

"Is there a way we can help?" Joey asked hopefully.

"Yes, I think there is," RJ nodded. "Meet me tomorrow afternoon and we'll go to Mrs. Monahoo's house."

"Do you really think that's a good idea?" Joey asked with a frown. "She already wants to talk to your parents."

"I think it'll be fine," RJ nodded.

Chapter 11

The next afternoon RJ and Joey walked over to Mrs. Monahoo's house. She was just stepping out on the porch to take her dog for a walk. When she turned around and saw RJ she squinted at him to be sure it was him.

"What are you doing here?" she asked. "I thought I asked you not to bother me anymore."

"I'm sorry Mrs. Monahoo," RJ began. "I feel so bad about the way I've frightened you, and I was hoping you'd let me make it up to you."

"Make it up to me how?" Mrs. Monahoo asked suspiciously.

"Well I thought maybe you'd let Joey and I walk your dog for you," RJ suggested with a smile. "What do you think?"

"Oh?" Mrs. Monahoo was stunned. "Sure," she nodded as she handed over the dog's leash. "Then I won't have to miss my favorite show!"

"Great, we'll be back in a little bit," RJ said warmly.

"What a fine young man you are," Mrs. Monahoo said with a smile. "And you smell much better too. You took a bath didn't you?" she asked sweetly.

"Uh, yes," RJ nodded a little. He saw no point in arguing about his hygiene. As they walked away from Mrs. Monahoo's house Joey was smiling.

"That was kind of you RJ," he said.

"It's not kindness, it's poo prevention," RJ explained sternly.

"Speaking of poo prevention," Joey said and snapped his fingers. "Who is picking up the poo?"

"Well," RJ cleared his throat. "I'm the one holding the leash, so I guess you'll have to be the one who cleans up the poo."

"What?" Joey gasped and shook his head. "No way! That is the worst smelling poo ever!"

"Joey, it's important to do things for others," RJ was explaining as they walked down the sidewalk. As they argued over who would be the pooper scooper, RJ was certain of one thing. At least there wouldn't be any more surprise piles in the middle of the sidewalk. Mystery solved!

RJ – Boy Detective #5

Mr. Pip Is Missing!

PJ Ryan

RJ – Boy Detective #5: Mr. Pip Is Missing!

Chapter 1

Summer in the city was one of RJ's favorite times. There was always something fun to do to escape the summer heat.

He liked to duck into the air conditioned museums. He liked to run through the open fire hydrants on the side streets. He even played a little hopscotch and kickball with some of the kids on the block. Joey had lots of water guns that he liked to fill up and chase RJ around with.

But by far the most important part of summer was knowing exactly when the ice cream truck would roll through. The ice cream truck, Mr. Pip's, covered a lot of blocks, so if RJ wasn't downstairs waiting for it, it would be too late to catch it.

It was hard to miss, dark red with big pictures of ice cream cones and popsicles on the side.

RJ and Joey would do odd jobs for the residents in the apartment building like taking out the trash or watering plants to earn enough extra money to get an ice cream just about every day.

So no matter how much fun they had playing in the fire hydrant or chasing each other with water guns, they always made sure that they were outside of the apartment building at exactly two-thirty when the ice cream truck would come.

Every day at exactly the same time, Mr. Pip's truck would roll by playing the craziest tune. It sounded like a mixture of twinkle-twinkle and take me out to the ball game. It was a funny song, but it was one that made RJ very happy.

Mr. Pip had the best ice cream in the entire city, and he only came around in the summer.

Mr. Pip himself was a man with a bald head, a big bushy brown mustache and an Italian accent that made everything he said sound a little funny. RJ liked him and looked forward to seeing him each day.

"Alright Joey, we have to hurry," RJ said as he glanced at his watch. "Mr. Pip will be here soon."

They shut off the video game they had been playing and took the elevator from the floor of RJ's apartment to the lobby. RJ and Joey waved to Hensely who waved back and slipped RJ a dollar.

"A mint crunchie please," he whispered. Hensely would never be caught buying from the ice cream truck while he was on duty, but RJ always made sure to help him get a treat.

"You got it," RJ grinned. Joey tagged right along beside RJ. Joey was younger than RJ. During the summer he spent most of his time with RJ because his mother was at work. He was a good little detective's assistant and RJ didn't mind him hanging around.

Chapter 2

As they waited out front of the apartment building that RJ's parents managed, they chatted about their plans for the rest of the summer.

RJ was hoping to spend some time with his cousin Rebekah. She lived in a small town and was nearly as good a detective as he was. Whenever they got together they usually found a mystery to solve.

RJ glanced at his watch and frowned as he looked up and down the street. There were plenty of cars and taxis on the road, but no sign of Mr. Pip.

"Weird," RJ mumbled as his watch showed that it was almost three. "Mr. Pip is never late," he narrowed his eyes.

"Maybe there was traffic," Joey pointed out. But he was starting to get nervous too. He didn't like to miss out on his ice cream.

RJ and Joey waited until fifteen minutes after three for Mr. Pip to show.

"I guess he's not coming today," RJ said. He was very surprised to say the words. He had never said them before.

"But I'm starving," Joey moaned and rubbed his belly.

"My Mom has some popsicles in the freezer," RJ offered, but he knew it wouldn't be the same. Mr. Pip had the best ice cream in the whole city!

Just as they were turning to walk back into the apartment building they heard a familiar sound. It was the music from Mr. Pip's ice cream truck. RJ spun around happily to greet the truck. The red truck with the pictures of ice cream on its side did roll past, but when RJ waved to flag it down, it just kept rolling.

"Mr. Pip!" RJ shouted and waved his hand faster.

"Mr. Pip!" Joey screamed and ran down the sidewalk after the truck. But again it just kept driving. RJ was stunned as he watched the truck turn down the next block. That was not even the correct route. RJ was very confused, and he was sure that something was wrong.

"We need to follow that truck," RJ said with determination. Joey nodded and shoved his hands into his pockets.

"So we can get some ice cream," he said sternly.

"No," RJ rolled his eyes and shook his head. "So we can find out what happened to Mr. Pip and why the truck has a new route."

"Oh yes, that too," Joey nodded and then whispered. "But really so we can get ice cream, right?"

"Joey," RJ sighed and patted the top of his head. "We'll get ice cream later. Now hurry up and let's see if we can catch up to the truck!"

The two ran after the ice cream truck, but when they reached the side street that it had turned down, there was no sign of it. Only the faint tinkling of its song could barely be heard. The music was too far away for RJ to figure out where it was coming from.

"We lost him," RJ sighed and snapped his fingers. "But we won't lose him tomorrow."

He adjusted his detective's hat on his head and squared his shoulders. He had a real mystery to solve, and he was going to solve it as soon as he could. Otherwise, summer might be ruined for everyone!

That night as RJ tried to sleep he was worried about Mr. Pip. He wondered if he had sold his truck to someone. Was he sick? Did he have a replacement driver?

Maybe someone had stolen the truck. RJ was sure that had to be it. Someone had stolen Mr. Pip's truck, and now they were going to have to get it back for him.

All the thoughts that floated through his mind worried him. None of them made much sense.

He just hoped that Mr. Pip was okay. He couldn't imagine summer without Mr. Pip's ice cream truck. Just the thought of it made it very hard for RJ to sleep.

Chapter 3

RJ woke up very early the next morning. He packed a bag with waters, binoculars and snacks. He wanted to make sure that he had everything he and Joey might need to track down the ice cream truck.

When he rode down in the elevator, he was one of the first people in the apartment building that was up and about. RJ's parents managed the building and he knew just about everyone who lived there, including Hensely, the doorman, who got up even earlier than RJ did.

"Good morning RJ," he said as RJ walked out into the lobby.

"Good morning Hensely," RJ replied though he couldn't quite smile. He was still too worried.

"Why are you up so early?" Hensely asked curiously.

"Joey and I are working on solving a mystery," RJ explained. "Something is going on with Mr. Pip's ice cream truck."

"I hope it's nothing serious," Hensely said with a frown. "Let me know if there's any way that I can help."

"I will," RJ said with a nod. He was a very skilled detective, but this was one mystery he was a little nervous about. If he couldn't figure out what was going on with Mr. Pip, he might never get to taste that amazing ice cream again. Outside of the apartment building he met up with Joey. He was yawning, but he was there.

"Why did we have to get up so early?" he asked sleepily.

"Because a mystery never sleeps," RJ said firmly. "Besides, I want to see if the truck drives by at any other time during the day."

"Alright," Joey sighed. "Anything for ice cream."

"I just hope we can find out what happened to Mr. Pip," RJ said with a grim frown. "One thing is for sure, he would never let kids miss out on their ice cream."

They staked out the block and asked everyone they ran into about Mr. Pip's ice cream truck.

"Have you purchased any ice cream from him recently?" RJ asked one teenager in a scruffy black bandana with a skateboard tucked under his arm.

"Sure I buy from Mr. Pip all the time. But not the past couple of days," he scratched his head. "I haven't' seen the truck around."

"Thanks," RJ nodded and moved on to an older woman who was sitting on a bench at the bus stop. "Excuse me ma'am," RJ said politely as he walked up to her. "I was hoping to ask you a few questions about Mr. Pip's ice cream truck."

"Oh that nuisance," she sighed and rolled her eyes. "That noisy truck comes by here every day! Who needs to eat ice cream every day?" she asked.

"I do," Joey said and held his hand up in the air.

"As skinny as you are, I'd say so," the woman chuckled and winked at Joey. Joey smiled charmingly. RJ sighed and pulled out his notebook.

"I was wondering if you've noticed anything different about the truck lately," RJ said calmly.

"Only that it hasn't been around much. I catch my bus at two forty-five every day. I'm always a little early just in case the bus comes earlier. So every day I have to put up with that Mr. Pip's truck," she sighed and shook her head. "It's been nice to not hear it the past few days."

"Thanks," RJ sighed as he closed his notebook. He didn't seem to be getting any new information from anyone. The woman stood up to walk over to the corner store. When she did, she left a pamphlet on the bench beside her.

"Look at this," Joey said as he picked it up with a giggle. "Broccoli on a stick," he held it up for RJ to see.

"What?" RJ's eyes widened as he looked over the pamphlet.

The pamphlet didn't just have a picture of broccoli on a stick. It also had a picture of a carrot with sprinkles. There was a celery stalk that was covered in peanut butter. On the cover of the pamphlet it proudly stated:

Veggie Pops much better than ice cream!

RJ's eyes widened at that. "Well I like vegetables just fine, but let's be honest here," RJ said with a scowl. "Better than ice cream? They're two very different things,"

He studied the pamphlet thoughtfully and then tucked it into his pocket.

"Keep your eyes peeled Joey, the truck could come through at any time."

"I am!" Joey said as he watched the passing traffic. "I just hope that this time it'll stop! I really want some ice cream."

"Me too Joey," RJ said sadly. "Me too."

Chapter 4

No one RJ and Joey talked to knew anything about the change in Mr. Pip's pattern. It was as if most of them didn't notice that Mr. Pip's truck came through at the same time every day. But then, why would they? RJ never saw too many adults running after the ice cream truck. That's when it hit him.

"We need to talk to kids!" RJ announced with a snap of his fingers. "Let's see if we can find some on the next block," RJ suggested. Joey followed him to the next block where a group of kids were playing ball on one of the side streets.

"Hi guys," RJ called out as he walked up to them.

"Hi RJ," one of the taller kids called back. RJ knew him from school, his name was Doug. "Want to play?" he offered.

"Not today Doug," RJ said with a shake of his head. "We're on official detective business."

"Oh," Doug nodded. "Must be important."

"I think it is," RJ agreed. "Have you noticed Mr. Pip's truck coming through here at the wrong time?"

"Sure have," Doug nodded and a few of the other kids did too. "I also saw it's not Mr. Pip driving the truck. It's some younger guy, I don't know him."

"Really?" RJ frowned. "Do you know what he looked like?"

"He had a big yellow shirt on and dark brown hair," Doug said as he looked toward the street. "I kept running after the truck and he just kept on driving. I was pretty upset and so was my little sister," he added as he tilted his head toward a curly haired little girl still pouting on the curb. "If he doesn't show today, I'm going to be in real trouble."

"Don't worry," RJ said firmly. "We're on the case!"

Just as RJ had jotted down the description of the man that Doug saw, they all heard the sound of Mr. Pip's truck rolling down the street.

"It's here, it's here!" both Joey and Doug's little sister cried out. "Stop him, stop him!" they both demanded.

RJ and Doug looked at each other and then ran out toward the street waving their hands in the air. But the big red truck that they knew was Mr. Pip's truck kept right on driving. It looked different too. It didn't have any pictures of ice cream on the side of the truck. In fact it didn't have any pictures on it at all.

"Strange," RJ mumbled.

"Ice cream," Joey moaned.

"I'm mad!" Doug's little sister stomped her foot.

"Well we can get you guys some ice cream from the store," RJ suggested.

"It's not the same," Joey and Doug's little sister both said at the same time.

"Let's follow him," RJ said as he grabbed Joey by the elbow. He and Joey began running in the direction that the truck was driving, but the truck was going pretty fast.

"Hurry up," RJ shouted over his shoulder to Joey. The truck turned down a side street, then another. It almost seemed like it was trying to get away from RJ and Joey.

"RJ!" Joey gasped out as he slowed down. "I can't run anymore, my legs are tired."

"Mine too," RJ breathed heavily as he slowed down. There wasn't much that they could do to keep up with a truck.

"That's it," RJ sighed. "That's all we can do for today. Let's try again tomorrow."

As RJ and Joey trudged home, RJ had a sinking feeling that something was really wrong with Mr. Pip.

Chapter 5

The next day RJ and Joey were waiting for the truck, but this time they had their skateboards with them, so that they could keep up.

"Stay close to me," RJ warned Joey. "And no going in the street!"

"I'll be careful," Joey promised as he put one foot on his skateboard. There was so much traffic that it was hard to spot the truck, especially since it didn't have the pictures of ice cream on it anymore. It also wasn't playing its usual mixture of songs. RJ still spotted its dark red color in the middle of the traffic jam.

"It's not going to get away from us this time," RJ smirked as the slow traffic meant that they should be able to keep up. The truck rolled along slowly in the traffic.

RJ and Joey crossed the street at the crosswalk, carrying their skateboards. Then they walked right up beside the truck. It was idling as it waited for the traffic light to change.

When RJ peered in through the window, he saw the man that Doug had described. The man did not see him. He was looking at the traffic. He even blared his horn. Mr. Pip would never do something unfriendly like that. The man in the driver's seat was definitely not Mr. Pip.

"I don't think he's selling ice cream from that truck," RJ said darkly as he stared through the window at the driver. The driver turned to look directly at RJ. RJ stared right back at him, letting him know that they were on to him. Then the light changed.

As the truck rolled forward, RJ could still see the driver looking back at him. "I think he's up to something and I'm going to find out exactly what it is including what he's done with Mr. Pip."

"Great," Joey nodded as he rolled his skateboard back and forth on the sidewalk. "But first can we please get some ice cream?" he begged.

"Are you even listening to me?" RJ grunted. "He's not selling ice cream."

"Ugh, I'm not going to make it," Joey groaned. "I've got to get one of those peanut butter crunch bars!"

"I know," RJ said sadly as he patted Joey's shoulder. "I know."

Chapter 6

RJ sat at his desk in his room. He had his notebook out and was going over some of the information he had jotted down. He was sure there was something he had overlooked. He was trying to figure out all the possibilities of what might have happened to Mr. Pip.

He had looked up Mr. Pip on the Internet, hoping to find his address, but he wasn't listed, at least not as Mr. Pip. So he was stuck back at square one.

As he began flipping through his notebook he came across the pamphlet that he had picked up off of the bench. RJ stared down at the strange versions of vegetables that were pictured in the pamphlet. Then he picked it up to look at it a little more closely.

As he flipped through the glossy pages he noticed how the vegetable treats seemed to look a lot like the ice cream treats that Mr. Pip had been selling from his ice cream truck.

RJ shook his head with confusion and flipped the pamphlet over to tuck it back into his notebook. When he did he noticed there was a picture of a man on the back of the pamphlet. RJ stared down into the eyes of the man who had been driving Mr. Pip's truck.

"Oh no," he gasped out as he realized what this meant. Not only did this man own Mr. Pip's truck, but he wasn't selling ice cream at all anymore. He was selling vegetable treats!

Did that mean there would never be another Mr. Pip's ice cream treat sold from that big red truck? RJ didn't want to believe it, but it all began to make sense as he flipped through the pamphlet again.

That would be why he didn't slow down when RJ was calling him. He didn't have any ice cream to sell. It would also explain why he had taken the pictures of ice cream down from the side of the truck.

But what it couldn't explain, was how Mr. Pip could ever let something so terrible happen. Where was he?

Didn't he care about the kids who waited for him every day of the summer? Didn't he know that he was just as important as the sun in the sky and the water in the fire hydrants?

RJ was sure that if Mr. Pip knew what was really happening with his ice cream truck, he would not be happy about it, just like RJ was not happy about it at all.

Chapter 7

The next day RJ thought about looking into the mystery a little more, but he just couldn't bring himself to do any investigating. Instead he sat sadly on the curb outside of the apartment building.

He didn't have any of his detective equipment with him anymore. He was feeling down about what had happened to Mr. Pip's truck and the ice cream that had been the best part of summer.

He was so sad and distracted that he didn't even hear Hensely walking up behind him.

"Hey chum, why so glum?" Hensely asked as he crouched down on the curb beside RJ. "I don't think I've seen you this down in the dumps since they canceled that detective show that you liked."

RJ looked up at Hensely with a deep frown. "Oh this is much worse," he said with a heavy sigh. "Mr. Pip is gone forever Hensely," RJ said sadly. "I couldn't solve the mystery in time."

"Are you sure about that?" Hensely asked as he looked at RJ. "Sometimes things look dreary, but there just might be a silver lining if you look close enough!"

RJ looked up at Hensely for a long moment. He adjusted his detective's hat on his head. He thought of his younger cousin Rebekah and whether she would give up in a situation like this.

"You just might be right Hensely," RJ suddenly said as he stood up from the curb. "I'm not ready to give up on Mr. Pip. Maybe he isn't ready to give up on us either!"

"That's the spirit," Hensely smiled. "Now get to work RJ, and get us back our ice cream!" he slapped RJ lightly on the back. "If anyone can do it, it's you!"

Chapter 8

RJ nodded his head with a stern smile. He marched down the sidewalk determined to find the truck.

Soon Joey was marching behind him. Before he knew it, Doug, his friends and even his Doug's little sister were marching right behind him. Kids they didn't even know joined the march as soon as the whispers reached them that they were trying to bring back Mr. Pip's ice cream truck.

RJ spotted the dark red truck and began walking quickly toward it. It turned down the side street and RJ expected it to disappear again. But this time he was quick enough to see it turn into a small garage.

RJ and the group that was marching behind him crossed the street at the crosswalk as the garage was closing behind the truck.

RJ paused in front of the business that owned the garage. It had a large fancy sign hanging above it. Each letter was a different color and was in the shape of an animal.

"Designs by Delaney," he read quietly as he looked up at the sign. It seemed like an odd place to hide an ice cream truck.

"What do you think he's doing in there?" Joey asked, surprising RJ as he didn't even know that Joey was there. He had been so determined that he didn't notice all of the people that began marching behind him.

When he turned to look at Joey and found a big group of kids behind him, he was very surprised.

"Wow, what are you all doing here?" RJ asked with wide eyes as he looked at all of the faces who were waiting eagerly to find out what RJ would do next.

"We're here to get Mr. Pip back," Doug said as he crossed his arms. "We know that you're a great detective RJ. If anyone can solve this mystery, it's you."

"Thanks guys," RJ said with a wide smile. "You stay out here. I'm going to check out what is going on inside."

"I'm coming with you," Joey said firmly. "Just in case there's ice cream," he added in a whisper.

"Joey," RJ rolled his eyes but he let the younger boy follow after him.

Chapter 9

When RJ opened the door to the small shop and stepped inside he noticed all of the art and paintings on the wall. "Hello?" he called out into the empty shop.

"Hello?" a voice called out from the garage. "I'm with a customer, I'll be right there!" a woman hollered from the garage. RJ frowned as he knew that whoever was in the garage was responsible for Mr. Pip's truck being taken over by vegetables.

He moved quietly toward the door of the garage and stuck his head inside. What he saw was very surprising. Not only were there no pictures of ice cream on the side of the truck anymore, now there were pictures of vegetables!

"Ugh!" RJ smacked his forehead at the sight. Vegetable were great, but not on an ice cream truck! "Where is Mr. Pip?" RJ asked as he stepped into the garage.

"Young man you're not allowed back here," the woman who must have been the owner of the shop said.

"It's okay Delaney," the driver of the truck said as he stepped around it to face RJ. "It's just one of Dad's loyal customers," he explained.

"Dad?" RJ asked with surprise. "You're Mr. Pip's son."

"Yes I am," the man said as he held out his hand to RJ. "I'm Philip Pip."

"Nice to meet you," RJ said politely and shook the man's hand.

"And I'm his daughter, Delaney," the woman said as she shook RJ's hand as well.

"Is something wrong with Mr. Pip?" RJ asked nervously.

"Nothing is wrong," Philip promised him. "It's just that he's decided to retire. He asked me to take over his ice cream business."

"Oh," RJ said quietly. "Is that why you are turning it into a vegetable treat truck?" he asked with a frown.

"I get it, you don't approve," Philip laughed. "But kids don't eat enough vegetables! If you would just try some, I bet you would like them."

"I do like them," RJ replied with a frown. "But I like ice cream too. And Mr. Pip's ice cream truck had the best ice cream around. All school year we look forward to having it in the summer. You have to understand what it's like to look forward to something."

"I do," Philip nodded as he looked over at Delaney. "But there is plenty of ice cream in the world. I thought having some vegetable treats would be a much better summer snack."

"See Philip, this is what I tried to explain to you," Delaney said as she crossed her arms. "Kids want Dad's ice cream, not vegetable treats. If he knew that you were going to change things like this, I just don't think he would have retired."

"You mean there might still be ice cream?" Joey asked hopefully as he stepped out into the garage behind RJ.

"This is Joey," RJ said as he rested his hand on Joey's shoulder. "He's just a young boy, who looked forward to Mr. Pip's ice cream every year. He eats his vegetables too, don't you Joey?"

"Oh yes I do," Joey nodded quickly. "I know I can't just eat ice cream all of the time."

"Hm," Philip frowned. "Well now I'm just not sure what to do. I've already put new designs on the truck."

"I think I might have an idea," RJ said as he smiled at Philip. "Why not do both?"

"Both?" Philip asked with surprise.

"Sure, sell ice cream and vegetable treats," RJ suggested. "That way kids get their ice cream and veggies too.'

"That's not a bad idea," Philip said slowly.

"I could add some ice cream designs on to the truck too," Delaney offered. "Then everyone could have the treat they want."

"I think that might just work," Philip smiled and nodded. "Let's do it! Mr. Pip's Ice Cream and Vegetable Truck!"

"Perfect!" RJ laughed. "And I can even tell you who your first customer will be."

Chapter 10

At exactly two-thirty that afternoon, RJ stood beside the bench at the bus stop. The woman he had spoken to the day before was sitting there as well. Soon they both heard the odd music of Mr. Pip's ice cream truck.

"Oh here we go again," the woman huffed and shook her head as the truck rolled slowly past the bench. "As if kids need ice cream every day," she mumbled. Then she noticed the tasty vegetable treats that were painted on the side of the truck.

"Well look at this," she said with a smile. "Hello!" she stood up and waved her hand at the truck. "Stop please!"

"Allow me," RJ said politely. He ran up beside the truck waving his hand. "Stop! Stop!" he called out. Soon all of the kids in the neighborhood, including Joey, were gathered around the truck. RJ took a broccoli pop to the woman waiting on the bench for the bus first. She smiled as she took a bite of it.

"Delicious!"

Joey got his peanut butter crunch bar. Doug's little sister got her ice cream cone. RJ was finally able to bring Hensely his ice cream treat. RJ was happy that he had figured out the mystery of the disappearing ice cream truck, but he was even happier that summer could get back to its normal fun.

From that day on, even though it had a new driver, Mr. Pip's ice cream truck was also Mr. Pip's vegetable truck and everyone was treated to the summer snack of their choice.

RJ – Boy Detective #6

Where Is Hensely?

PJ Ryan

RJ – Boy Detective #6: Where Is Hensely?

Chapter 1

RJ closed and locked his apartment door behind him. His parents were managers of the whole building and they lived on the top floor. RJ knew just about everyone who lived in the building.

He was headed out to meet his friend Joey at the small park a few blocks away. Joey was a few years younger than him, but he and RJ were good friends because RJ would look after him after school.

He was almost to the elevator when one of the tenants stepped out of her apartment and stopped him in the hallway. Mrs. Baker frowned as she glanced up and down the hallway before looking back at RJ.

"RJ, have you seen Hensely?" she asked with concern in her voice. Hensely was the doorman of the apartment building and had been ever since RJ moved in.

"I'm sure he's downstairs," RJ shrugged. "Do you want me to get him for you?" he asked. Hensely was always at his post, from dawn until dusk, and sometimes he stayed even later. He liked to keep an eye on the apartment building and the people that lived in it. He was always looking out for RJ and Joey too.

"No, he's not," Mrs. Baker shook her head firmly. "When I came in from my jog this morning he wasn't there. Then when I went downstairs to get some coffee, he wasn't there either. Now Mr. Chumley said that he has been paging Hensely from his room for over an hour and Hensely isn't answering."

Hensely knew there were some elderly residents in the building, so he gave them a special number to call him on if they needed help getting from their apartments downstairs or if they had groceries or something to carry.

"That's odd," RJ frowned as he adjusted his detective's hat on his head. "Hensely is always downstairs at his post."

"I know," Mrs. Baker said her eyes wide. "That's why I thought maybe you knew where he was. I'm going to help Mr. Chumley, but if you see Hensely please let me know."

"Yes ma'am, I will," RJ promised her as he walked down the hallway.

It was very odd for Hensely not to be at his post, especially when someone needed him. RJ rode the elevator downstairs, the whole time wondering where Hensely could be. Maybe he was ill? RJ hoped not.

When he reached the lobby he stepped out, expecting to see Hensely. Instead he saw an empty lobby. It was a large open space with the mailboxes for the residents on one wall and a big front desk on the other wall where people could leave packages or stop and talk to Hensely for a little while.

But today Hensely wasn't standing by the front desk. He also wasn't standing by the front door waiting to open it. RJ walked over to the restrooms in the lobby. He stuck his head inside the men's room.

"Hensely, are you in there?" he called out. There was no answer.

RJ frowned and walked back out into the lobby. He arrived just in time to hold the door for Ms. White who was struggling to keep control of her yapping fluffy poodle. It was a tiny little dog, but strong. RJ knew because he had offered to walk FooFoo once as a way to earn a little extra money. The dog had nearly pulled him right down the street.

"Oh thank you RJ," Ms. White gasped as she struggled through the door. "Hensely is usually here with a treat for FooFoo. I don't know where he is today and she's very upset!" Ms. White looked pretty upset too. Everyone was used to the little things that Hensely did to help them each day.

"Sorry Ms. White," he said and reached into his pocket hoping to find a crumb or a cracker saved there. "I don't have any treats."

"Oh it's okay," Ms. White huffed as she was nearly dragged over to the elevator by her precious puppy.

RJ watched until he was sure they were safely on the elevator, then he took a look around the lobby again. RJ walked up to the front door and looked outside thinking Hensely might have gotten in a conversation with the man at the magazine stand.

He didn't see Hensely in front of the building or at the magazine stand either. When he turned back inside, he noticed something very strange.

There was a round black hat on the floor in the middle of the lobby, a very familiar round black hat.

Chapter 2

RJ peered down at the black hat. It was the same hat he had seen Hensely wear every day since his family had moved into the building. RJ had never seen him without it. Now it was in the middle of the lobby floor, with no sign of Hensely.

"Very suspicious," RJ said as he picked up the hat. When he picked up the hat he found a long white feather underneath. "Even more suspicious," RJ narrowed his eyes. He pulled a tissue out of his pocket and picked up the feather. He looked at it very closely.

"Whatcha got there RJ?" Joey asked from just behind him. RJ was surprised by Joey's loud voice and dropped the feather and the hat.

"Joey!" RJ growled as he straightened up and picked up the feather and the hat again. "Don't sneak up on me like that."

Joey smiled innocently. "How could I sneak up on the best detective in the city?" he asked with a wink. RJ had a reputation for being a detective. He wanted to be a detective when he grew up, but decided he couldn't wait that long, and had been investigating mysteries for quite a few years.

When he began looking after Joey in the afternoons, Joey became his assistant detective, and the two had solved several mysteries together.

"There's no time for joking around Joey," RJ said grimly as he held up the hat and the feather. "Hensely is missing."

"Hensely?" Joey asked with surprise. "But he's always here."

"I know," RJ frowned. "But the only sign of him today is his hat and this feather," he added as he held up the feather. "Where in the world did it come from?" RJ wondered as he looked at the feather closely.

"Maybe," Joey thought for a moment and then raised his eyebrows. "A bird?"

"Ha, ha, of course a bird Joey," RJ replied and scrunched up his nose with annoyance. "But what would a bird be doing under Hensely's hat?" he asked and shook his head.

Hensely was very friendly with all of the pets in the building, but RJ had never seen him with a bird. "Do you know if anyone has a pet bird in the building?" he asked Joey thoughtfully.

"Mr. Polk has one on the fourth floor," Joey said quickly. "But it's just a parakeet and it's very small. That feather is bigger than Mr. Polk's entire bird."

"Hm," RJ rubbed his chin. "Well maybe someone got a new pet that we don't know about," he suggested. "We should find out," he added as he looked up from the feather.

When he did he noticed a man standing in the corner of the lobby. He was dressed in all black, with a very tall black top hat. When RJ spotted him, the man ducked into the door that led to the stairway.

"Why would he take the stairs?" RJ asked himself with confusion. "He's wearing a nice suit. He'll be all sweaty by the time he gets to the floor he wants."

"I've never seen him here before," Joey added suspiciously. "He looks a little odd," he pointed out.

"I agree," RJ said thoughtfully. "Do you think we should follow him?" RJ smirked as he already knew they would.

"I do, detective RJ," Joey nodded. RJ tucked the feather into his pocket and they crept toward the stairs.

Chapter 3

Very quietly they followed the man up the stairs. RJ could hear the sound of his footsteps echoing through the stairway. He put his fingers to his lips to remind Joey to walk very quietly.

RJ wanted to see what floor the man got off on. He didn't have to wait long. The man stopped at the second floor and opened the door. RJ and Joey quickly followed after him. Before the door could close all the way behind the man, RJ caught it with his hand. He peered through it and watched as the man walked right to the elevator.

"Maybe he changed his mind about the stairs?" RJ whispered to Joey. "Maybe he realized he didn't want to get his nice suit messy."

"Maybe," Joey nodded. They stepped out into the hall just as the elevator doors were sliding shut.

"Look at that!" RJ cried out as he pointed to the direction the elevator was traveling in. "He's going right back down to the lobby!"

"Weird!" Joey declared, and RJ had to agree.

"Let's see if we can catch up to him," RJ suggested and ran back toward the door that led to the stairs. RJ and Joey pounded quickly down the stairs. They weren't worried about making too much noise anymore.

When they reached the bottom of the stairs and threw open the door to the lobby, the elevator doors were just closing. There was no sign of the man in the tall black top hat.

"Very, very, strange," RJ sighed as he walked across the lobby to the elevator.

"And still no sign of Hensely," Joey pointed out grimly. His hat was still in the middle of the lobby floor. RJ picked it up and set it on the front desk so that it wouldn't get trampled on.

"Well I know Hensely would never leave his post, not unless something terrible happened. So we need to get to the bottom of this, and fast," RJ added urgently. Wherever Hensely was, RJ knew he was anxious to get back to his post.

"Maybe we should check his apartment?" Joey suggested.

"Good idea Joey!" RJ snapped his fingers. Hensely lived in the apartment building and RJ knew where he kept the spare key for his apartment.

Chapter 4

When they arrived at Hensely's apartment, RJ lifted the small welcome mat he had in front of his apartment door. He found the key and unlocked the door.

His parents had very strict rules about going into the tenant's apartments when they weren't home, but RJ was sure that they didn't apply when Hensely was missing. Once they were inside, RJ and Joey began calling for Hensely.

"Are you here?" Joey called out as he headed for the kitchen.

"Hensely?" RJ shouted toward the bedroom. "Are you sick?" he pushed the bedroom door open enough that he could peek inside. Hensely's bed was neatly made. There was no sign of anything being out of place.

When RJ turned back toward the living room, Joey was still in the kitchen.

"Look he must have had breakfast," Joey said as he pointed out the bowl and spoon in the dish drainer. The kitchen was neat as a button without anything out of place either.

"So he can't be out getting a bite to eat," RJ said with a frown. "And he isn't sick either."

"But he's not here," Joey frowned. "I don't see anything that could tell us where he is either," he added.

He and Joey walked back out into the living room, which was also very tidy. RJ sat down on the couch to think for a moment. When he did, he spotted a flyer on the table. It was the only thing that seemed out of place, as there were no other papers just lying about.

"Look at this Joey!" RJ gasped as he picked up the flyer. "Astounding Aristotle," he read off of the flyer. Underneath the bold letters was a picture of a man in a black suit with a very tall top hat. "Does he look familiar?" he asked Joey as he held up the flyer for Joey to see.

"That's him!" Joey gasped too. "That's the man we saw in the lobby. Why would Hensely have a flyer about a magician?"

"Hm," RJ frowned as he studied the flyer. "He must have been looking at this today. He never leaves things out. It says here that he's playing two shows today at the theater down the block. Maybe Hensely was planning to go to his show?"

"Even if he was planning to go, the first show isn't for another hour," Joey pointed to the show times on the flyer.

"And I'm sure he wouldn't leave without telling anyone," RJ shook his head. "Something doesn't add up."

"Well," Joey whispered as he looked at RJ. "You do know what magicians do."

"What do you mean Joey?" RJ asked with a frown.

"I mean, they make things disappear," Joey pointed out with wide eyes.

"Wrong," RJ said sternly as he rolled up the flyer and stuck it into his pocket. "They play tricks on people. They don't actually make anyone disappear."

"All I'm saying is that Hensely went missing, and then we saw this Astounding Aristotle sneaking around," Joey explained with a shrug.

"You have a good point," RJ agreed with a scowl. "I think we should find out just what Aristotle was doing in our building this morning. What do you think Joey, want to see a show?"

"Yes I do!" Joey clapped his hands. "I love magicians!"

"Then you're going to get to meet one," RJ said with determination. "Hensely had this for a reason. We need to find out what this magician knows about his disappearance."

Chapter 5

When they left for the show, Joey had his magician's hat on. It made him look much taller than he was. The theater was very crowded and they didn't have tickets.

"I hope it's not sold out," RJ frowned as he walked up to the ticket booth. The woman behind the glass was just starting to close her window.

"Two for Astounding Aristotle please," RJ said as he stood in front of the window.

"Oh I'm sorry hon but we're all sold out," the woman shook her head. "You should have gotten here a lot sooner. Astonishing Aristotle is very popular."

"What about his evening show?" Joey piped up.

"That one is sold out too," she frowned. "Sorry guys, I guess you'll have to see him next time he's in town."

"He's only here today?" RJ asked with surprise.

"Yes he'll be leaving town tomorrow," the woman said. "He'll be back later this year though."

RJ sighed as she closed her window. He knew they couldn't wait until later in the year to talk to Astounding Aristotle. He was their only lead into Hensely's disappearance.

"I guess we have to give up," Joey said with a frown.

"No sir," RJ adjusted his detective hat on his head. He smoothed down the red hair underneath. He straightened the collar of his shirt. "We do not give up."

In all the years that RJ had been a detective he had never given up on a mystery. He wasn't going to start now.

"Then what are we going to do?" Joey asked with confusion.

"We're going to go to the show," RJ replied with a light smirk.

"How are we going to do that?" Joey asked as he followed RJ around the corner of the theater.

"We're going to be part of it," RJ explained. He turned to look at Joey. "Do you think you can act like a dummy?"

"I'm not a dummy," Joey said with wide eyes. "RJ why would you say something so mean to me? I thought we were friends!"

"Not that kind of dummy," RJ rolled his eyes. "Like a wooden dummy."

"Oh!" Joey laughed and then frowned. "Well, I guess so," he shrugged.

"Good, then we are going to get into the show. But first, we need to change."

Chapter 6

RJ and Joey ran back to the apartment building. Joey ran to his apartment and RJ rode the elevator all the way up to his. He changed into the tuxedo he had worn to his aunt's wedding.

Once he was dressed he put on his detective's hat. It was his dressy detective's hat, the black and white checks went well with his tuxedo.

When he met Joey downstairs, Joey was dressed in the tuxedo he had worn when he dressed as a spy for Halloween.

"Very nice," RJ said with a nod. "Now we have to hurry or we'll be late for the show."

Once they reached the theater they ran around behind it to the service entrance. This was where the staff, actors and actresses entered the theater.

"Are you ready for this Joey?" RJ asked him. "Remember, you're a dummy."

"I'm not-"

"Not that kind of dummy," RJ growled. "Get with it Joey, this is for Hensely!"

"For Hensely," Joey nodded and straightened his bow tie.

As they stood outside the entrance, a security guard spotted them.

"What are you two doing here?" he demanded as he walked over to them. RJ had his hand slipped up the back of Joey's tuxedo jacket.

"Two?" he laughed a little and shook his head. "It's just me and my Dummy."

Joey shot him a look of annoyance. The security guard laughed.

"Wow he looks so real," he said with a grin. "Can I touch him?"

"Sure," RJ said with a smile. "Just don't tickle! And careful, he bites," he added. The security guard laughed again and poked Joey right in the forehead.

"Wow! He even feels real," he said with a shake of his head. "What will they think of next?'

"Ha ha, I don't know," RJ shrugged. "But I'm late, I have to get inside."

"Hm," the security guard said as he looked over the list of names on his clipboard. "I don't see anything about a dummy. What's your name?"

"I won a contest," RJ explained quickly. "At my school. Astounding Aristotle knows all about it. But if I don't get in there I'm going to miss the show. Then I'll be in trouble, and you'll be in trouble and we don't want that, do we?" RJ raised an eyebrow.

"Alright, alright," the security guard nodded. "Go on."

RJ sighed with relief and pretended to carry Joey toward the door.

"Hey kid!" the guard called out from behind RJ. RJ froze. He was sure that the security guard had figured out that he wasn't supposed to be there.

"Yes?" he asked as he looked over his shoulder.

"Nice hat!" he smiled. RJ adjusted his detective's hat and smiled back. As he walked into the back entrance of the theater he knew he had only made it through one hurdle.

There was still a chance that Astounding Aristotle would not even talk to him.

"Do I still have to pretend to be a Dummy?" Joey asked out of the corner of his mouth.

"No it's okay," RJ said as he waved to him to hurry. "We have to find the magician's dressing room before he gets out there on stage."

"Okay," Joey hurried after him. It was hard to find the dressing rooms because the hallways were dark. The show was going to start soon. Finally they came to a dressing room with a big golden star on the door. RJ smiled.

Chapter 7

"This must be it," he said as he stopped in front of the door.

"Let's see if he's there," Joey said and knocked on the door. RJ's eyes widened as he had planned to just spy on the magician, but Joey's way worked much better. Astounding Aristotle opened the door.

"What do you want?" he asked gruffly as he looked down at Joey.

"Uh, uh," Joey stammered as he looked up at the magician.

"We want to know what you've done with Hensely!" RJ said loudly from behind Joey. "We know you had something to do with it! We saw you at the apartment building this morning!"

"I don't know what you're talking about little boy," Astounding Aristotle said as he glared at RJ. "But I don't like to be accused of things. How did you two even get back here?" he demanded. "You are going to be in serious trouble if I find out you sneaked in."

"Uh," RJ lowered his eyes and cleared his throat. "All we want to know is where Hensely is," he said firmly. "Then we'll leave you alone."

"Astounding Aristotle, show time!" a woman called from the side of the stage.

"I have to go on, I don't have time for this," Astounding Aristotle said grimly. "If you two don't have tickets, then you need to leave the theater."

"Wait, please," RJ called after the man as he began stalking toward the stage. "Can't you tell us where Hensely is? He's our friend!"

Chapter 8

Astounding Aristotle looked back over his shoulder with a frown before he stepped through the curtains and out on to the stage. The large audience cheered as the announcer announced his presence over the loud speaker.

"Ladies and gentlemen, the amazing, the astonishing, the astounding, Aristotle!"

"Hmph, more like mean Aristotle," Joey grumbled as he stood beside RJ. "I can't believe he wouldn't tell us the truth."

"If he won't tell us the truth, that must mean he's hiding something from us," RJ said firmly. "We're going to have to find out what's going on the old fashioned way."

"What do you have in mind?" Joey asked.

"We're going to look in his dressing room for some clues," RJ said as he glanced around to see if anyone was watching.

Once he was sure that the coast was clear he opened the door to the dressing room. He and Joey slipped inside. RJ closed the door behind him.

The dressing room was dark because Aristotle had turned out the light when he left. As RJ was fumbling around for the light switch, Joey was staring straight at something covered up with a blanket in the corner.

"What's that?" Joey stammered as he heard a loud squawk come from under the blanket. RJ found the light and turned it on.

"Never mind that," RJ said sternly. "We have to find a clue before someone catches us."

He began looking through the papers on the desk in the dressing room. Joey was still staring in the direction of the strange squeak.

"Look at this," RJ said with surprise as he picked up a picture that he had found in the middle of all of the papers.

"What is it?" Joey asked without looking away from the blanket covered object in the corner.

"It's a picture," RJ explained as he walked over to Joey with it. "Look, it's Hensely," he said as he showed him the picture. "At least it looks like him, only younger."

"You're right," Joey said as he looked at the picture. "And that looks like Astounding Aristotle standing next to him."

"I think it is," RJ said with a nod. "So now we know that they know each other," RJ said thoughtfully.

"But how?" Joey wondered. "Look on the back of the picture, sometimes people write things on the back."

RJ flipped over the picture and gasped when he saw what was written on the back.

"Hensely brothers," he read. "Astounding Aristotle and Hensely must be brothers!"

"Wow that would be so cool to have a brother that's a magician!" Joey said with wide eyes.

"But it still doesn't explain where Hensely has gone," RJ said with a frown. "And why did Aristotle act like he didn't even know who Hensely was?" he shook his head. "Something isn't right."

"Maybe they're not close," Joey said with a frown. "I know some brothers fight a lot. Maybe Hensely and Aristotle were angry at each other."

"Huh," RJ said softly. "So if they were angry at each other, maybe he and Hensely got in a fight at the apartment building this morning."

"But what about the feather?" Joey asked with a frown.

"And why would Hensely leave his hat behind?" RJ asked with confusion.

As they thought about this and looked at the picture of the Hensely brothers, they heard another loud squawk.

Chapter 9

"What is that?" Joey asked with surprise.

"Let's see," RJ said and crept close to the cage. He tugged on the blanket until it pulled off of the object it was hiding. Underneath was a large bird cage. Inside was a large white bird.

"Look!" Joey pointed at the bird with wide eyes. "Its feathers are the same color as the one we found!"

"Yes they are," RJ said and pulled the feather he had found in the lobby of the apartment building out of his pocket. He picked up a feather from the bottom of the bird's cage. It was the same color and just about the same size.

"So this bird must have been in the lobby this morning too," RJ said with a frown. "But how would one of its feathers get under Hensely's hat?"

"Oh no," Joey gasped as he looked around the room, then at the bird, then at RJ. "Do you know what this means RJ?"

"No," RJ replied honestly. "What does it mean?"

"Astounding Aristotle is a magician. He was angry at Hensely, his brother. He went to see him this morning. There's only one way that a feather could get trapped underneath of Hensely's hat!" Joey was talking so fast that RJ was only getting more and more confused.

"Joey what are you talking about?" RJ asked with surprise.

"I think that's Hensely!" Joey said as he pointed at the bird in the cage.

RJ stared at Joey, then he stared at the bird in the cage.

"Joey, that's not possible," RJ said with a shake of his head.

"Duh, magicians know magic!" Joey stomped his foot. "Isn't it obvious? Astounding Aristotle was angry at Hensely so he turned him into a bird! That's why he was afraid we'd see him at the apartment building. That's why he didn't want to talk about Hensely a few minutes ago! He's afraid we'll figure it out and he'll get in trouble."

"I don't know," RJ said hesitantly. "Magicians play tricks Joey, they don't actually perform magic."

"That's what you think," Joey said as he crossed his arms. "What do you think poor Hensely thinks?" he asked as he looked at the bird in the cage. "Don't worry Hensely, we'll get you out of there," Joey said as he tried to unlock the cage. It had a padlock on it, so there was no way to unlock it. RJ looked at the bird. The bird looked back at him.

"Is that really you Hensely?" he asked softly.

"Hensely, Hensely," the bird said back as it walked back and forth on its thick wooden perch.

"Oh no!" RJ gasped. "It really is him. What are we going to do?"

"I don't know," Joey shrugged a little. "Give him some crackers?" he suggested.

"No, we're going to make Astounding Aristotle turn Hensely back into a person!" RJ said sternly.

Chapter 10

"What are you two doing in here?" a voice said sharply from the doorway of the dressing room.

RJ's eyes widened as he turned to see Aristotle standing in front of them with his wand in hand.

"Oh no!" Joey ducked behind RJ. "Please Astounding Aristotle don't turn us into birds!" he squeaked out.

"What?" the magician asked with a frown. "I hope you didn't upset my bird!"

"Don't you mean your brother?" RJ asked boldly.

"What?" the magician asked again with a bigger frown. "What exactly is going on here?"

"I'd like to know the answer to that too," another voice said from behind Aristotle.

"Hensely!" RJ said with surprise as he saw Hensely standing behind Aristotle.

"RJ, Joey, what are you doing here?" Hensely asked with confusion.

"We thought you were the bird," Joey tried to explain, but he was very confused too.

"How could I be a bird?" Hensely laughed.

"Well we found your hat, with a feather underneath," RJ explained with a frown. "Then we found out your brother is a magician, and-"

"Okay, okay," Hensely laughed again. "I wanted this to be a surprise, but I guess it's not anymore. Yes, my brother is a magician," he smiled and patted his brother's shoulder.

"We thought you were missing," RJ pointed out. "What happened?"

"Well, Artie here came by to see me this morning. He wanted to show me a new trick he was doing with his bird. But his bird wasn't feeling the best," Hensely explained and lowered his voice. "The trick did not go as planned."

"It was not my fault," Aristotle said with a pout. "His tummy was upset."

"Let's just say I had to get my jacket cleaned," Hensely said with a wink. "I was in such a hurry to get the stain cleaned before it set, my hat must have fallen off. I didn't even notice."

"But why did you run from us in the lobby?" RJ asked Aristotle.

"I was embarrassed," Aristotle admitted. "Hensely is my big brother and I would always show him my tricks. But they never seem to work out right when he's watching.

Pippa was supposed to sit on my brother's head, under his hat, for part of the trick. But she got scared and flew out from under his hat, and well, left some droppings behind," he added in a whisper.

"Ew," RJ cringed. Joey laughed.

"But the bird was saying Hensely," Joey pointed out.

"I taught him a few words, like our last name," Aristotle explained. "I'm sorry if I scared you two."

"I just came in to pick up these tickets for this evenings show," Hensely explained. "I can't wait for you guys to see my little brother in action! He's the best magician ever!"

"Thanks Hensely," Aristotle beamed.

RJ and Joey were happy they were going to get to see the show. They were also happy that Hensely was not a bird.

Night Noises

BOOM

PJ Ryan

RJ – Boy Detective #7:
Night Noises

Chapter 1

In a very quiet room, in a very quiet apartment, in a very quiet apartment building, a very quiet boy was sleeping. At least, he was quiet while he was sleeping.

He was having one of his favorite dreams. He liked to read about detectives that had worked throughout history. He liked to imagine that he was part of their detective team.

Sometimes he was lucky enough to have a dream about working with one of these famous detectives. It always made him very happy when he woke up and remembered getting to work with one of history's great detectives. At least he woke up happy when he got to have the whole dream.

This particular night he was dreaming about working with Sherlock Holmes. They had just found a mysterious set of footprints that led up to an old run down mansion. RJ was eager to find out what was inside, but before he could find out, he heard a loud boom!

It made him jump out of his skin and nearly fall out of his bed. It took him a moment to realize that he was awake. His room was dark and quiet. He wondered what could have woken him up. He didn't have to wonder for long before he heard another very loud Boom!

RJ rolled out of his bed with a yelp. He crawled across his floor and out into the hallway of his family's apartment.

"Mom? Dad?" he called out nervously as he edged his way down the hallway. He was afraid the booms might have been an explosion of some kind. He had never heard anything so loud before.

"Mom? Dad?" RJ called out again as he stood outside their bedroom door. RJ thought he was too old to be going to his parents when something scared him, but he told himself that he just wanted to make sure they were okay.

"RJ?" his mother asked as she opened the door. "Are you okay?"

RJ shifted from one foot to the other. "Did you hear that Mom?" he asked.

"Hear what?" his father asked sleepily from the bed. "Do you know what time it is RJ?" he demanded. "Go back to sleep, please!"

RJ's mother patted the top of his head, which was covered in his black and white 'sleeping' detective's hat.

"It must have been a bad dream sweetie, I'll take you back to bed," she said and hugged him. RJ shook his head.

"No it wasn't a dream," he said firmly. "I was awake when I heard it. It was a great big 'Boom'," he insisted.

"Sometimes when we have a very realistic dream it's hard to know what happened when we were sleeping and what happened after we woke up," his mother explained as she guided him back to his room. "Just try to go back to sleep RJ, everything will make more sense in the morning."

"Alright," RJ sighed as he stepped back into his room. He was sure that he had been awake when he heard the loud sound, but maybe his mother was right. He had been in the middle of a good dream after all.

Maybe the boom had been part of the mystery in the room. Maybe the old mansion had exploded. He lay back down, hoping that he would get to finish his dream.

Chapter 2

The next morning RJ woke up feeling very tired. He forced himself to get ready for school. He loved going to school, but not when he would rather be sleeping. He yawned his way through breakfast.

Then he boarded the school bus. He almost fell asleep on the bus on the way to school. All through school he kept thinking of the sound he had heard.

No one else seemed to have heard it, at least no one said anything about it. He was beginning to believe what his mother had said, that it had just been part of his dream.

He hadn't been able to finish his dream, sadly, but at least he had gotten a little bit of sleep.

When he stepped off the school bus and waited at the corner for Joey's bus to arrive, he was pretty sure that he had been fooled by his own dream. Joey hopped down off of his school bus. He met RJ's eyes.

"Did you hear that boom last night?" he asked with a huge grin.

"What?" RJ replied, surprised that someone else had heard it. "You heard it too?" he asked.

"Of course I did," Joey laughed. "Who could have missed it? I fell right out of my bed!"

"No one else heard it," RJ said with a frown. "My Mom said it must have been a dream."

"No way," Joey shook his head firmly. "I know it wasn't a dream because I was still awake. I was trying to see the stars through my bedroom window. But it's hard because of all the lights. So I thought maybe if I stayed up extra late there would be enough lights out that I would see some."

"Did you?" RJ asked curiously.

"No of course not," Joey sighed. "I fell out of my bed!" he reached up and rubbed at the back of his head. "When I fell, I did see a few stars though. I don't think they were the same as the ones in the sky."

"Probably not," RJ laughed. "Well I'm glad someone else heard it. But I have no idea what it might have been."

"I don't know either, but it was loud. I was a little scared to go back to sleep. But I didn't hear any more booms all night. Did you?" Joey asked.

"Not one," RJ shook his head. "Maybe it was a car backfiring. Sometimes that sounds like a boom."

"Maybe, but it would have to be a very big car," Joey laughed.

That afternoon they stayed inside to play some video games. It was kind of cloudy outside and there wasn't much to do. RJ tried to focus on the game, but his mind kept wandering back to that loud boom he had heard in the middle of the night. He just couldn't stop thinking about it.

Chapter 3

When he tried to sleep that night, he thought of the loud noise that had woken him the night before. He hoped he wouldn't hear it again.

When he closed his eyes he tried to think of quiet things…soft raindrops, the rustle of leaves, the swish of the slide when he slid down it. He was soon sound asleep. He wasn't asleep for long, however, before he was suddenly awake.

He heard something very odd. Screeeech. It didn't sound like a bird or an animal. It sounded like nothing he had ever heard before. It sounded like metal against metal, and it made all of the hairs stand up on the back of his neck.

His eyes opened wide. He pinched his arm to make sure that he was awake. He even sat up in his bed to make sure that he was awake. Then he heard the sound again. Screeeech.

RJ jumped right out of his bed. He wasn't going to let this noise pass him by. He ran to his parents' room and knocked on the door.

"Mom, Dad," he called through the door. "Wake up!"

"RJ, what is it?" his mother asked impatiently as she opened the door.

"I heard a noise again!" he announced as his father grumbled from his bed.

"Go back to sleep RJ. You're way too old for this! I have to work in the morning."

"But listen, you'll hear it," RJ said sternly.

"RJ," his mother said as she steered him back toward his bedroom. "We live in the city. You're bound to hear strange noises in the middle of the night. Not everyone keeps the same hours. Maybe there is someone moving around in the apartment downstairs. You have to just do your best to ignore it."

"No Mom," RJ insisted. "It wasn't that kind of noise. It was different," he explained. "It was loud, and it sounded like metal being twisted."

"Well there's construction going on down the block," she reminded him. "Maybe one of the machines is swinging in the breeze, or maybe someone is working extra hours. Just try to sleep, okay?"

RJ frowned as she stopped beside his bedroom door. "You believe me, don't you Mom?" he asked.

"Always RJ, but that doesn't mean that your father and I don't need sleep. So please, unless it's an emergency, try not to wake us up," she met his eyes sternly.

"Alright Mom," RJ nodded and headed back to bed. He lay awake, hoping he would hear the noise again before his parents had a chance to fall asleep. But it was quiet enough to hear a cricket, if there were any crickets. When he finally fell asleep he was very disappointed.

Chapter 4

The next morning he was sleepy again. He made his way to the bus stop, barely keeping his eyes open. He made his way through his classes, barely hearing his teachers. By the time he got off of the bus he was ready for a nap.

While he waited for Joey he yawned, and yawned and yawned some more. When Joey stepped off of his bus he looked just as tired.

"Did you hear that last night?" he asked with a yawn.

"Yes," RJ sighed and shook his head. "But of course my parents didn't."

"My Mom didn't hear it either," Joey frowned. "I think she thinks I'm having nightmares."

"If I wake up my Dad one more time he's going to ground me, I know it," RJ frowned. "We need to figure out what is going on. I don't think I can get through one more sleepless night."

"Me either," Joey agreed. "But how are we going to figure it out?'

"Well, it's Friday night, see if your mom will let you stay the night at my place," RJ suggested. "Then we can sit up and listen for the sounds."

"Good idea," Joey said with a nod. "But I have one question for you. Will there be ice cream?"

"There is always ice cream," RJ replied with a smile.

Chapter 5

Once RJ and Joey had permission to have a sleep over they stocked up on the usual sleep over supplies. They had flashlights, cookies and the ever important scary movie.

RJ picked one that wasn't too scary because of Joey. And maybe a little bit because the noises he heard during the night were scary enough. RJ and Joey camped out in RJ's room to wait for the night to come.

"Do you want to take a nap now?" RJ asked as he handed Joey a cookie. "So that you'll be awake later?"

"I'll be awake," Joey said firmly. "I want to find out what all the noise is about."

"Me too," RJ agreed.

They ate their cookies. They watched their movie and they were both sound asleep before the streetlights even came on. They hadn't been sleeping well for the past few nights so they just couldn't stay awake.

RJ's Mom checked on them and found the half-empty box of cookies, the movie still playing and the flashlights left on. She turned off the flashlights and the movie and took the cookies to the kitchen.

In the middle of the night, RJ heard a very strange sound. It sounded like footsteps above his head. Very loud footsteps. He was so scared by the sound that he could barely open his eyes. Beside him in his sleeping bag, Joey whimpered.

"Did you hear that?" he whispered to RJ.

"I heard it," RJ whispered back nervously. He slowly opened his eyes. He heard it again. Thump, thump, thump. It was so loud that if it was footsteps, they had to be the biggest feet ever.

"Like elephant feet," RJ whispered.

"Scary elephant feet!" Joey cringed and ducked his head under the edge of his sleeping bag.

"We have to see what's causing it," RJ said firmly. He was trying to be brave. He climbed out of his bed and pulled on his slippers. Joey wriggled out of his sleeping bag and pulled on his shoes.

They picked up their flashlights and turned them on. The flashlights made the bedroom seem very spooky.

They crept quietly out of RJ's room.

"Shh," RJ said. "We can't wake my parents up."

Joey nodded and they silently opened the door. The hallway was empty and dark. Everyone else on the top floor was sleeping. RJ and Joey crept toward the sound, which seemed to be coming from above them.

"Do you think there might be an elephant on the roof?" Joey whispered. "Maybe all that noise is a circus!" he sounded a little excited by the idea. "Maybe there's a secret night time circus on the roof!"

"That's ridiculous!" RJ said with a huff. "Think clearly Joey. If there was a circus on the roof, don't you think we'd hear the lions roar?"

"Oh," Joey nodded a little. "Good point."

"Not to mention the clowns," RJ reminded him. "Clowns can never be quiet."

"That's true," Joey agreed. Stomp, stomp, stomp, stomp! They heard the noise right above their heads.

"We need to see what's going on up there," RJ said sternly. He reached for the door that led to the flight of stairs that led to the roof. He started to turn the knob. Before he could turn it, the knob started turning under his hand.

"Oh no!" RJ gasped as he backed up and bumped into Joey. "There's someone in there!"

"Eek!" Joey gasped. "Maybe it's the elephant."

"Elephants can't open doors-" RJ said with exasperation.

Chapter 6

"What are you two doing out here?" RJ's mother said sharply from just behind them.

"Eek!" Joey said again and ducked behind RJ.

"Mom, we heard a noise and there's someone in the stairwell!" RJ said urgently as he looked into his mother's annoyed eyes.

"It is not safe for you two to be wandering the halls RJ. You should know better than this. Joey's Mom trusted us to look after him. How do you think she would feel if she knew that you were out roaming the halls in the middle of the night Joey?" she asked crossly.

Joey hung his head. "Sorry," he murmured.

"But Mom, there's someone in the stairwell!" RJ insisted.

"Oh RJ," his mother rolled her eyes. "I've told you time and time again, these are dreams you're having!" she opened the door to the stairwell. RJ cringed as he had no idea who might be on the other side.

"See?" his mother said as she took his flashlight and shined it into the stairwell in all of the dark corners. "There is no one here!"

RJ's eyes widened as he looked inside the empty stairwell. He was sure that someone had been there a moment ago.

When he looked up at the stairs leading to the roof, he thought he saw the back of a shoe disappearing into a shadow. But he knew his mother would not believe him.

"Sorry Mom," RJ said sadly.

"Just get back to bed, both of you," she said and walked them back to the apartment.

Once they were alone in RJ's room again he began pacing back and forth.

"I know what I heard," RJ said firmly.

"But your Mom said-" Joey began to say.

"They don't believe me," RJ sighed. "But that doesn't mean there isn't something going on. We need to find out what it is."

"Can we find out tomorrow?" Joey yawned sleepily.

"Yes we better wait until tomorrow," RJ nodded. He knew if his mother caught him out in the hallway again she would be very upset.

Chapter 7

The next night they slept over at Joey's apartment. It was on a lower floor. RJ and Joey were more careful to stay awake so that they wouldn't miss any of the noises.

Once Joey's mother was asleep, RJ and Joey listened very closely. At first they didn't hear anything but the blaring of horns and people talking on the street below.

But after an hour passed, they began to hear a very strange sound. It was quieter than the others Joey had heard. It was there though. Clank, clank, clank, clank. RJ jumped up.

"Did you hear it?" he asked Joey.

"I heard it," Joey nodded and picked up his flashlight. They sneaked out into the hallway.

"It's coming from above us," RJ said and pointed to the door that led to the stairwell. "Let's see if we can find out what it is once and for all!"

Carefully RJ opened the door to the stairwell. They crept inside, and began following the sound up the stairs. RJ was nervous, but he tried not to show it.

"Keep up with me Joey," he whispered to his younger friend. Joey nodded and held tightly to his flashlight.

RJ and Joey followed the quiet clanking sound up the stairway. The higher they got on the stairs, the louder the clanking sound became. RJ glanced over at Joey. Joey winced and pointed to the next flight of stairs.

It sounded like the clanking was coming from one more flight up. RJ began creeping up along the stairs. When they reached the last flight before the roof, RJ was really starting to get nervous. He had never been on the roof at night before, at least not alone.

It was a large space that could be used for parties and had a small garden for the entire apartment building on it. But it was strictly off limits to RJ without someone being with him, and especially at night.

Still that clanking sound was loud enough to make him sure that it was coming from the roof.

"Should we go up there?" Joey whispered as he leaned closer to RJ.

"I'm not sure," RJ admitted. He was usually very brave, but he wasn't sure that going on the roof was a good idea. After all, they still had no idea what was making the sounds that they were hearing.

Was it an animal of some kind? Was there a strange machine on the roof that would vaporize them all? Before RJ could decide all of the lights turned off in the stairway.

"Eek!" Joey cried out and ducked behind RJ. The lights in the lower stairways were still on, but the flight leading to the roof was completely dark.

"Don't worry Joey," RJ said as he pulled out a flashlight and flicked it on. It was very bright, but it barely made a dent in the darkness that flooded the stairway. That clank, clank, clanking was still filling their ears, even though the lights had gone out. "We have to keep going."

They carefully climbed the rest of the stairs. RJ opened the door to the roof and took a deep breath.

Chapter 8

When RJ stepped out on to the roof he was surprised to discover a large object hidden beneath a larger cloth. He stood in the doorway of the stairwell, staring at the cloth. He wasn't sure if it was hiding something terrifying, or something very silly.

Maybe it was an art project that one of the tenants had been putting together.

"What do you think is hiding under there?" Joey asked RJ in a whisper.

"I don't know," RJ replied and took a few steps forward. He heard the clank, clank, clanking coming from underneath the cloth. "But I'm going to find out," he said bravely.

He wasn't going to spend one more sleepless night without figuring out what it was that was keeping him awake. "Here, help me pull the sheet off," he said.

RJ grabbed one end of the sheet and Joey grabbed the other. Together they tugged it carefully off of what was hiding underneath.

"What is it?" Joey whispered as the sheet fell away. Underneath was a large piece of machinery. RJ couldn't quite tell what it was. It was round and black. It was standing straight up and down on the roof, and was too wide for RJ to put his arms around.

Clank, clank, clank, came the sound they had been hearing all night.

"Where is that coming from?" RJ wondered and walked around the side of the barrel shaped object. When he walked around to the other side, he let out a loud yelp. There had been someone under the sheet as well!

A short man, that RJ recognized from the building. His name was Mr. Smithe, and he had moved in a few months before. He was short and slim and had been completely hidden by the large object that they uncovered.

Chapter 9

"What are you doing?" RJ demanded as the man banged carefully on a piece of metal connected to the large object. He was using what looked like a wrench to lightly tap at a hinge.

Mr. Smithe didn't answer. In fact he didn't even turn around. It was as if he didn't notice RJ standing there at all. RJ's heart beat faster. Could he be a zombie? Could he be hypnotized?

One thing was for sure, he was the one making that clank, clank, clanking sound.

"Mr. Smithe!" RJ said louder as he put his hands on his hips. "Do you know what time it is? That's much too noisy!"

Mr. Smithe still didn't look at him. He just kept banging the wrench against the hinge. Then he stopped and put the wrench down. He picked up a can of spray.

"What are you doing with that?" RJ asked nervously as Mr. Smithe raised the can into the air. He took a slight step back and bumped right into RJ.

"Ah!" Mr. Smithe cried out when he bumped into RJ. He pushed down on the can by accident, and the spray shot out all over the hinge before Mr. Smithe dropped it on the ground. He spun around fast and glared at RJ.

"What are you doing up here?" He demanded. "Do you know what time it is?"

RJ stared at him with wide shocked eyes. As he stared Mr. Smithe pulled earplugs out of his ears and tucked them into his pocket. That was why he hadn't heard RJ!

Joey peeked out from around the large object to see what was happening. When he saw Mr. Smithe and RJ staring at each other he gulped.

"I know what time it is," RJ said flatly as he looked at Mr. Smithe. "Do you?"

"Excuse me?" Mr. Smithe asked with a frown. "I am an adult and I can be on the roof at any hour I please."

"But not making all of these loud noises," RJ pointed out as he shook his head. "What have you been building up here? Does my father know about this?"

"Shh," Mr. Smithe frowned. "No he doesn't know about it and you're not going to tell him either!" Mr. Smithe glowered at RJ. RJ was a little afraid. He didn't know Mr. Smithe very well and it was clear that they had interrupted whatever his plan might be. Perhaps he felt that they had seen too much.

"We won't tell anyone," RJ promised as he looked at Mr. Smithe.

"Good," Mr. Smithe's glare relaxed into a wide smile. "Because it's a surprise for everyone."

RJ relaxed too and smiled back. "What is it?" he asked as he looked more closely at the object.

"It's obviously a signal to space aliens," Joey said with a shrug as he stood beside RJ.

"A what?" Mr. Smithe laughed. "No it isn't a signal to space aliens. It is a surprise, like I said," Mr. Smithe reminded them. "Now you two should be in bed."

"We would be if we could sleep!" Joey said with a stomp of his foot. "Every night we're woken up by these loud noises."

"Oh dear," Mr. Smithe frowned. "I guess I didn't realize how loud I was being. When I first brought this up here I lost my grip on it and dropped it. I know that had to be a very loud!"

"It sure was," RJ agreed as he recalled the first loud boom.

"Then when I had to tighten the bolts and screws I had to use my drill, and that made an awful screeching noise," Mr. Smithe explained as he shook his head.

"It was very awful," Joey agreed.

"Then when I tried to tilt this big guy, I found the hinges weren't moving very easily. So I was rocking it back and forth to try to get it to move. That probably sounded odd from downstairs," he said thoughtfully.

"It sounded more than odd," RJ pointed out with a shake of his head. "It sounded like there were elephants running around up here."

"Oh no," Mr. Smithe chuckled. "So sorry about that. But no elephants up here, just my big surprise."

"What is it? What is it?" Joey asked bouncing from one foot to the other. Mr. Smithe looked at them both and frowned.

Chapter 10

"Well since it seems I've been keeping you up for a few nights, and you went to all the trouble of solving this mystery for yourselves, I guess it wouldn't hurt to show you," he smiled as he turned back to the hinge that was covered in spray.

"Let's just see if this worked," he said quietly and pushed on the hinge. The big barrel shifted and aimed at an angle toward the sky. "Perfect," he sighed. "Come here boys," he gestured for Joey and RJ to come closer.

"Are you sure it's not an alien signal?" Joey asked nervously. "Because I don't really want them knowing where I am!"

"It's not an alien signal," Mr. Smithe said firmly.

"Just look through here," Mr. Smithe said as he pointed to an opening on the barrel. Joey shook his head and took a step back. But RJ did his best to be brave. He stepped forward and peered through the opening on the barrel.

What he saw was amazing. He could see hundreds of stars spread across the sky above them. He'd only seen stars so bright when visiting his cousin Rebekah in the small town she lived in.

"Oh Joey, you have to look," RJ said as he took a step back so that his friend could have a chance to look through.

"No aliens?" Joey asked nervously.

"No aliens," RJ promised him with a shake of his head. Joey sneaked up to the opening and peered through it.

"Wow!" Joey gasped. "Look at all those stars! I've never seen so many in one place before!" he said loudly.

"Shh!" Mr. Smithe murmured and laughed. "Don't want to wake up the whole building."

"I didn't think I could ever see stars in the city," Joey said as he stepped back from the object. "How did you do this?"

"Well boys, before I retired I was an astronomer," he explained. "I love this city but I missed the stars so much. So I built this super telescope. As I said though, I had a few problems putting it together.

I thought it would be something nice that everyone in the building could enjoy. I hope your parents won't mind," Mr. Smithe said with a frown as he looked at RJ. "I wanted it to be a surprise."

"They won't mind at all," RJ promised him with a smile. "But you have to tell them about the noises you were making up here. They thought I was having bad dreams."

"I'm really sorry that I kept you boys up," Mr. Smithe sighed. "I had the earplugs in to drown out the noise of the traffic. It makes it hard for me to concentrate. I guess I didn't realize how loud I was being."

"It's okay," RJ smiled as he looked at the large telescope. "You had a good reason!"

"Maybe you boys could help me reveal it tomorrow night?" Mr. Smithe asked. "Could you invite all of the residents of the building up here for a party tomorrow night?"

"Absolutely!" RJ agreed and Joey nodded quickly.

Chapter 11

After RJ and Joey actually got some sleep they woke up early the next morning. They marched up and down the halls of every floor of the entire apartment building, inviting all of the people that lived there to a party on the roof that night.

Everyone seemed pretty excited about the idea. RJ made sure to invite Hensely too.

"What's the party for?" Hensely asked curiously.

"It's a surprise," RJ grinned.

"Oh I'm sure you already figured it out," Hensely laughed.

"It's still a surprise for you though," RJ grinned. "You're really going to like it!"

"I'll be there," Hensely promised. RJ and Joey picked up some supplies for Mr. Smithe and helped move a few tables up to the roof. Once everything was all set the guests began to arrive.

Mr. Smithe showed them each how to work the large telescope. He even showed them how to find different constellations and planets.

"And, I'm sorry if I caused anyone any disturbance with all of my noise," Mr. Smithe added. RJ smiled up at his parents.

"See?" he said with a nod. "I wasn't having nightmares!"

"Well I think next time we'll believe you," his father said with a laugh, then took his turn at the telescope.

The Cheese Thief

PJ Ryan

RJ – Boy Detective #8:

The Cheese Thief

Chapter 1

RJ was very excited as he left his apartment. It was one of his favorite days of the week. Really, he liked them all, but this day was special.

Once a week, if RJ and his friend Joey both kept up with their homework and helped out around the apartment building, RJ's parents would give them twenty dollars to take to the pizza place and have a special dinner.

RJ's parents were the managers of the apartment building, so they knew all of the tenants. Tony, the owner of the restaurant, lived in the apartment building and RJ's parents knew him very well. They knew that RJ and Joey would be safe alone at his restaurant.

Every Saturday night Joey couldn't wait to get to the pizza place. By the time RJ stopped by his apartment to pick him up, he was barely able to stand still.

"Oh just think RJ," he gushed as he hurried out the door of his apartment. "Pretty soon we'll be chowing down on the most delicious pizza in the whole city."

"It's going to be great!" RJ agreed with a grin. As they rode the elevator down to the lobby of the apartment building he pulled a small hand held radio out of his pocket.

"Look what I found," RJ said as he showed it to Joey.

"Oh that's cool," Joey said and tilted his head to the side. "Is it broken?"

"Well right now it is," RJ sighed as he fiddled with the radio. "I put new batteries in it, but it hasn't worked yet. I'm trying to fix it," he explained as they stepped off of the elevator.

"Sometimes things are too broken to fix," Joey pointed out as they walked across the lobby.

"I know, I know," RJ grumbled as he fumbled with the handheld radio he was trying to get to work. He found it while investigating some strange sounds by the dumpster out back. The sounds had turned out to be rats, but he had also stumbled upon the old radio.

He was sure that if he could get it to work it would be a great thing to add to his collection of random things he liked to collect.

He was sitting on the curb in front of the apartment building fiddling with the radio.

"Hiya boys, off to pizza night?" the doorman Hensely asked as he held open the door for RJ and Joey.

"We'll bring you back a slice," RJ promised as he glanced up at Hensely with a smile. He was always looking out for RJ and Joey, so RJ tried to do the same for him.

"Sounds good," Hensely smiled and waved to them as they walked down the sidewalk to the next block where Tony's restaurant was. RJ kept fiddling with the radio, while Joey continued to gush about the pizza they would soon be having.

"We'll have two, or even three slices," he said with a delighted sigh. "And orange soda," he added and rubbed his hands together.

"Joey," RJ looked up at him with a frown. "You know what your Mom said about orange soda," RJ raised an eyebrow.

Joey was his friend, but RJ also kept an eye on him after school. He was a few years younger, and his mother had to work, so RJ would wait for him to get off the bus and they would spend their afternoons solving mysteries, or playing video games.

RJ wanted to be a detective when he grew up, but he couldn't wait that long. So he already worked as a detective to solve any mysteries that might come up.

"That I'm her wonderful son and she thinks I should have three glasses of it?" Joey asked with a wide smile.

"That it keeps you up all night," RJ corrected him with a laugh. "One glass, then it's water for you buddy."

"With lemon?" Joey asked hopefully.

"Only if you promise not to throw it at me," RJ narrowed his eyes as he recalled the epic lemon war they had the month before. Tony had not been too happy about that and RJ and Joey had to mop the floors with their bellies full of pizza.

"Wow, you used to be fun," Joey crossed his arms and kicked a rock off the edge of the sidewalk and into the street. RJ continued to fiddle with his radio.

He was looking forward to pizza night too. Tony saved them a table near the window so that they could see people walking by on the street. RJ liked to think about where they might be going, and why.

He was always looking for a new mystery to unravel. He was much better at solving mysteries than fixing radios.

"Is it time yet?" Joey asked as he danced from one foot to the other.

RJ glanced at his watch.

"Tony's not even open yet Joey," he pointed out. "He doesn't open until five. It's only four-thirty."

"Well can't we at least peek in the window?" Joey begged. "I'm starving!"

RJ rolled his eyes as he knew that Joey had probably just polished off a snack. Joey was very skinny, but he loved to eat anything he could get his hands on.

"I'm done trying to fix this anyway," RJ said with a grumble and tucked the small radio into his pocket.

Chapter 2

As they walked toward the pizza restaurant RJ noticed a slight chill in the air. It seemed the nights were getting cooler earlier than they normally did. He saw some people wearing jackets.

When they stopped in front of the pizza restaurant, he noticed one man wearing a very bulky jacket as he climbed into a truck and then sped off.

"Must not be used to the cold," RJ thought to himself as the coat was rather bulky. He had an aunt that lived in Florida and she was freezing if it was less than seventy degrees outside.

"See, it's still closed," RJ said as he pointed to the sign on the door of Tony's pizza place.

"Maybe if we knock," Joey said. RJ tried to stop him, but Joey had already knocked before he could.

"Ah Joey, hungry today, huh?" Tony laughed as he opened the door. "Go on in and have a seat. I just have to get the pizzas ready and you two can have the first one!" he smiled warmly at the two.

"Thanks Tony," RJ said with a smile. He and Joey walked over to their usual table. A few moments later, Tony came back out of the kitchen. He walked over to the table slowly. He had a deep frown on his face. RJ wasn't used to this as Tony was always very cheerful.

"What's wrong Tony?" RJ asked as he looked up at him.

"I'm sorry boys, no pizza today," Tony said as he walked past their table to the front window. He sighed as he turned the open sign to closed on the door of the restaurant.

"What?" RJ asked with a frown. "Why?"

"No cheese," Tony shrugged and sighed. "Our deliveries keep disappearing. I signed for them this morning, but when I went to make the pizzas, the cheese was gone! Now some people do like pizza without cheese, but most don't! No point in staying open if I can't feed my customers."

"I'm so sorry Tony," RJ said with a frown. "How are they disappearing?"

"Well, I'd like to say I misplaced them, or that they weren't delivered. But I'm pretty sure that they were stolen. I hate to think that, but there's just no other explanation."

"Who would steal cheese?" Joey asked with a frown.

"Hm, I wonder if Mouse is in town," RJ muttered under his breath. Mouse was a friend of his who lived in the same town as his cousin Rebekah. He got his name because of all of the mice he had for pets. With that many mice, he was sure it took a lot of cheese to feed them. But Mouse would never steal, that RJ was sure of.

"I really can't figure it out," Tony admitted. "I'm sorry boys. Maybe you can get some pizza rolls from the corner store."

"Pizza rolls," Joey scrunched up his nose. That didn't sound good at all compared to Tony's pizza.

Chapter 3

"Don't worry Tony," RJ said firmly. "Joey and I are on the case."

"Now boys," Tony said with a frown. "I know that you like to solve mysteries, but this is serious. If someone is stealing they are a real criminal and I don't want either of you getting involved."

RJ frowned. He hated to be told he was too young to do things. He knew that Tony meant well, but there was a lot more that RJ wanted to figure out.

Why would someone just steal cheese? He hadn't stolen the tomato sauce or the meat that went on the pizza. So why in the world would someone just need cheese.

"Sorry again boys," Tony sighed. "You should go so I can close up the shop. I will have lots of disappointed customers looking for pizza tonight."

RJ nodded as his stomach grumbled. He and Joey walked back to the apartment building from the pizza restaurant with their heads hanging low. When Hensely opened the door for them he saw how sad they were.

"What's wrong boys?" he asked as he closed the door behind them.

"Tony didn't have any pizza tonight," RJ sighed. "Someone is stealing his cheese!"

"Really?" Hensely asked with wide eyes. "Who would steal cheese?"

"A very large mouse," Joey suggested grumpily.

"Hm, well I suppose that's possible," Hensely chuckled a little. "Don't worry, I'm sure by the time the next delivery comes, they'll figure it out," Hensely patted RJ's shoulder. "Maybe just have Chinese tonight?"

"Chinese?" Joey groaned and shook his head. "That's worse than pizza rolls!"

As RJ and Joey rode the elevator up to RJ's apartment, RJ thought about what Hensely said.

"Hensely was right," RJ said with a slow smile. "The next delivery is key. If the cheese thief comes back, we can catch him!"

"Remember what Tony said," Joey said with a frown. "This is a real thief RJ, not just some kid who lost his football."

"And I'm a real detective," RJ insisted sternly. "We're going to figure this out for Tony. He's a good person and no one should be stealing from him. We'll be there for the next delivery."

"Okay," Joey nodded as they stepped off of the elevator. "But next time I'm getting orange soda, cheese or no cheese."

"Deal," RJ nodded as they stepped into RJ's apartment.

Chapter 4

Tony's next delivery was on Tuesday. It was in the afternoon right after RJ and Joey got out of school. RJ waited for Joey's bus, armed with a package of crackers.

"Here you go," he said before Joey could even announce that he was hungry. RJ adjusted his detective's hat on his head. He had one in every different color. He always wore one when there was a mystery to solve. Well, he always wore one no matter what. He even had one he wore to bed!

When they walked down the block to the pizza restaurant, RJ had his radio with him again.

"You still haven't fixed that?" Joey asked with surprise.

"It's not as easy as it looks," RJ said with a frown. "I can get it to turn on now, but all it picks up is static."

"Strange," Joey frowned. "Maybe there's something inside that's broken."

"Maybe," RJ nodded. When they reached the pizza restaurant it was still closed. RJ peeked around the side of the building. He could see a delivery truck in the parking lot behind it.

"Shh Joey, we can't let Tony know we're here," he warned him.

Joey nodded and whispered. "Don't forget about my orange soda though. Those crackers made me very thirsty."

"Alright," RJ said impatiently. "Hurry, before the delivery truck pulls away."

RJ and Joey crept along behind the building. They ducked behind the delivery truck when they heard voices. Tony was talking to the driver.

"Have you had any reports of any other thefts on your route?" Tony asked the driver as he signed the clipboard the driver handed him.

"Yes I have," the driver said as he took the clipboard back. "I don't understand it, but everyone seems to be having their cheese stolen. That's why I brought extra boxes of cheese for this round. I know it's not my fault the cheese got stolen, but I don't want my good customers going without the cheese they need."

"Thanks a lot John," Tony said with a smile. "I'm going to make sure that this cheese doesn't disappear."

"Good," John nodded and then tilted his head toward the stack of boxes on a dolly beside the truck. "Are you sure you don't want me to take it in for you?"

"No, it's fine," Tony waved his hand. "I can take it in."

Joey and RJ watched as John climbed back into the truck. They ducked behind the dumpster beside the truck before it pulled away. Tony picked up some small boxes of meat off of the stack on the dolly and then carried them into the restaurant through the back door.

"So far so good," RJ whispered.

Chapter 5

Just after John's truck pulled out of the parking lot, another truck pulled in. It didn't have any writing or pictures on it, but it looked just like the delivery truck John had been driving.

A man in a big thick jacket climbed out. He glanced around the parking lot and then ran toward the boxes that were left on the dolly. He lifted off some of the boxes until he reached the boxes of cheese.

"Hey!" RJ shouted when he saw the man snatch up the cheese. "Hey stop that! Those don't belong to you!" RJ shouted louder. The man looked up with surprise. When he saw RJ he ran to the back of the truck. He threw open the door and tossed the boxes inside.

"What's going on out here?" Tony hollered as he ran out of the back of the restaurant. But he was too late. The truck was already driving out of the parking lot. RJ and Joey started to run after it, but Tony yelled for them to stop.

"Don't ever chase after a vehicle!" he warned the two boys as he looked sternly at them. "You don't know if it will back up and you don't know what could happen!"

"Sorry," RJ sighed as he stared after the truck. "We almost caught him."

"I told you two, don't get involved," Tony warned them both. "Now RJ I'm going to have to tell your parents about this. Whoever is stealing this cheese could be a dangerous man and I don't want you to get hurt."

"I'm sorry Tony," RJ frowned. "But I did get the license plate number," he said as he showed him the number he had jotted down in his notebook.

"Good boy," Tony sighed as he looked at the number. "That should help the police. But if I see you hiding out back here again, you're going to be in big trouble, understand?" he looked at both RJ and Joey sternly.

"Yes Tony," they both said with frowns. RJ knew that Tony was just trying to keep them safe, but he was frustrated. He was very close to catching the cheese thief and now they were never going to be able to catch him.

As they walked back to the apartment building, Joey was disappointed. He still hadn't gotten his orange soda or his pizza.

RJ was fuming. He couldn't believe that someone would just walk up and steal the boxes of cheese. RJ didn't want the man who did it to get away with his crime. But what could he do if Tony said they weren't allowed in behind the restaurant again?

Then he remembered what the delivery driver had said about there being more thefts on his route.

"That's it," he smiled at Joey. "We can't watch Tony's deliveries, but we can watch the deliveries to John's other customers!"

"Will they have orange soda?" Joey asked with a scowl.

"Joey," RJ sighed and shook his head.

Chapter 6

The next day after school RJ and Joey spent the afternoon walking around the neighborhood. They stopped in different shops and restaurants to find out which of them were John's customers, whether they had any cheese stolen and when their next delivery was.

When they stopped in Gina's Deli she smiled at both of them.

"Hi boys," she said happily. "Want a pickle?" she grinned. RJ and Joey liked to stop in Gina's Deli for the dill pickles she kept in a jar on the counter.

"Sure!" Joey said with a grin. As Gina was getting them each a pickle, RJ asked her about the cheese thief.

"Have you had any cheese stolen?" he asked.

"Yes," she sighed and shook her head. "I had to go to the grocery store and buy some so I could serve sandwiches. It is a lot more expensive to buy cheese from the grocery store, than to buy cheese from John."

"Do you have a delivery coming up soon?" RJ asked curiously.

"Actually, I'm due for a delivery tomorrow," Gina nodded. "I'm going to make sure I get my cheese this time!"

"What time is your delivery?" RJ asked, hoping that Gina wouldn't ask him why he wanted to know.

"It's at four," she said with a frown. "Usually I get my deliveries in the morning, but since John is making an extra trip for me, he could only fit it in tomorrow afternoon."

"Well good luck, and thanks for the pickles," RJ said as he walked away from the counter.

"Thanks boys. Come back soon!" she waved to them as they walked out the door.

"Alright, tomorrow at four," RJ said firmly. "We're going to be waiting for that cheese thief."

Joey nodded, but he couldn't talk. He was too busy crunching up the pickle.

Chapter 7

The next day after school, RJ and Joey were hiding by the dumpster behind Gina's Deli. This time RJ had his radio with him to keep him busy while they were waiting. He was trying to tune in a station, but all he could pick up was static.

"RJ. I'm hungry."

"You're always hungry Joey," RJ reminded him.

"Can't I just go inside for a pickle?" Joey pleaded.

"No, because if you go inside then Gina will know that we're out here. She will get upset like Tony did," RJ reminded him. "This has to be a secret mission."

"Fine," Joey sighed.

RJ heard the rumbling of John's truck as it pulled up. Suddenly his radio crackled.

"Dropping off at Gina's," John's voice said over the radio.

"What was that?" Joey asked with wide eyes as he looked at the radio.

"It must be on a CB frequency," RJ said with surprise. "I thought it was just a regular radio."

"So you can hear what John says on his radio?" Joey asked with surprise.

"Let's listen," RJ said.

"Next up is the diner," a voice crackled back over the radio to John.

"I should be on time," John replied before climbing out of his truck.

While John and Gina were talking, RJ fiddled with his radio. He was wondering if he could pick up any other channels.

"He's there now," a voice crackled over the radio. "We should be able to get two more boxes."

RJ's eyes widened. "Joey, do you think that might be the cheese thief?" he asked.

"Maybe," Joey frowned as he listened closely to.

"We need it fast," a different man's voice crackled back over the radio. "No more close calls like last time!"

"Oh no, he's going to take Gina's cheese," RJ said with a frown. Just as he spoke, John's truck pulled out of the parking lot. Gina was looking over the boxes he had left behind. She wanted to make sure she had everything she needed.

Then the phone inside the deli began to ring. She looked around the parking lot quickly. Not seeing anyone nearby she hurried into the deli to answer the phone.

RJ stood up to guard the cheese, but before he could even cross the parking lot, the cheese thief's truck pulled in. The man was even faster this time. He ran around behind the truck, threw open the doors, then ran for the cheese.

"Stay right here," RJ said firmly to Joey as he tucked his radio into his pocket. "I'm going to stop him!" Joey nodded and stayed behind the dumpster.

RJ ran around the front of the truck to stop the man. But before he could reach him, the man had tossed the boxes into the back of the truck. He slammed the doors closed on the truck. RJ chased after it as Gina came running out of the deli to see what was happening.

"Stop!" RJ shouted at the truck. "Joey see if it's the same license plate number!" he shouted to Joey. But Joey didn't answer. RJ found out why when he saw Joey's face pop up in the back window of the truck that was driving away.

"Joey!" RJ shouted. "Oh no! He's got Joey!"

Gina was already calling the police as the truck sped off.

Chapter 8

The police arrived very quickly. RJ told them everything he knew. He was very upset.

"Don't worry son," the police officer said. "We'll find your friend."

RJ felt terrible. He knew that Joey's mom would be upset, his parents would be upset, and most of all he was upset. He should have made sure Joey was safe. As the officers were talking to Gina, the radio in his pocket began to crackle.

"There's a kid in the truck!" a voice said nervously.

"A kid? What?" the other voice shouted back over the radio.

"A kid jumped in the back of my truck!" the driver of the truck said. "I'm dropping him off on the corner."

"You can't, you might get caught!" the other voice said.

"I didn't agree to kidnapping," the driver said sternly. "You can make me do a lot of things, but I'm not doing this!"

"He's going to drop Joey off," RJ said quickly as he tried to get the officers' attention.

"Sure he will," one of them said with a smile. "No need to worry."

"No listen, I can hear him on this radio!" RJ insisted as he held the radio up.

"Look kid, you've done enough detective work for one day," the other officer said gruffly. "Just stay put so we can get this straightened out."

Chapter 9

RJ realized they weren't going to listen to him. He knew that if Joey got dropped off on some random corner he might get lost. He listened to the radio, but he couldn't hear the voices anymore.

He began to run off in the direction the truck had gone. After he ran for a few minutes, he could hear the voices again.

"You know what's going to happen if you get caught," the other man's voice warned the driver.

"And I'm not going to have some kid's Mom worrying about where he is," the driver argued back. "I'm stopping at Duncan and Turner, then I'll head your way."

"You better get here on time," the other voice said sternly to the driver. To RJ it sounded like the driver didn't want to listen to the person who was telling him what to do.

RJ ran as fast as he could to Duncan and Turner. He knew if he got too far from the truck he wasn't going to be able to hear what the driver was saying. Luckily he spotted the truck as it pulled over at the corner of Duncan and Turner.

The driver got out of the truck and opened the back door. Joey hopped right out, looking pretty scared.

"Get out of here kid," the driver said sharply.

Joey nodded and ran away from the truck. RJ was waiting for him. They both watched as the truck started to drive away.

"I dropped the kid off. Now I'm coming your way," the driver said into his radio.

"Are you okay Joey?" RJ asked and hugged him.

"Sorry I didn't listen to you RJ," Joey frowned. "I just thought I could stop him."

"So did I," RJ frowned. "And we're going to. Once and for all. Let's see if we can keep up."

He and Joey began running down the sidewalk to keep up with the truck.

"Outside now," RJ heard the driver say when he pulled up outside of a factory. A man stepped out of the side door of the factory.

"It's about time," he frowned. The driver opened the doors of the truck.

"This has got to be the last time Mikey," the driver said with a sigh. "I feel so terrible doing this."

"Well you don't have a choice," Mikey said with a glare. "You're going to keep stealing the cheese for as long as I need it. We can't make the cheese sticks without it."

RJ looked up at the sign above the factory. It said, "Mikey's Munchies" and had a picture of a cheese stick on it.

"Did you ever think about just buying the cheese?" the driver asked with a shake of his head.

"Why, when I can just get it for free?" Mikey laughed.

RJ growled. "He's stealing everybody's cheese to make cheese sticks!"

"I've had those cheese sticks, they're really good," Joey sighed. "I'm still hungry."

"Let's go Joey, hopefully the police will listen this time," he shook his head.

Chapter 10

When Joey and RJ ran back into the parking lot behind Gina's Deli, the police were still there.

"I found him!" RJ shouted to get their attention. The officers were very happy that Joey was safe. RJ told them about the factory, the driver and Mikey.

"If you hurry, you'll be able to catch them!" RJ said breathlessly.

"You know, you're a pretty good detective," one of the police officers said with a grin.

"Thanks," RJ said proudly.

"But you still shouldn't have been involved in this," the other officer warned.

"Right, sorry," RJ's smile faded. But he winked at Joey.

When the officers arrived at the factory the driver was still there. He told the officers that he had been forced to steal the cheese, because his brother, the owner of the factory didn't want to buy it. Joey and RJ were hiding behind one of the police cars and listening to them talk.

"I knew it was wrong to steal the cheese," the driver said sadly. "But Mikey told me that if I didn't he would never make another cheese stick. Have you ever tasted his cheese sticks?" he asked with wide eyes.

"They are good," one of the police officers nodded with a slight smile, but his smile faded fast. "But that's no excuse to steal. You're both under arrest!"

As the two men were taken off to jail, RJ was proud that they had been able to solve the mystery. However, when RJ and Joey got back to RJ's apartment, RJ's parents and Joey's mother were waiting for them.

"I think you boys need a break from detective work," RJ's father said sternly. "What you did today was very dangerous."

"I know," RJ frowned as Joey's mother hugged him.

"No detective work for a week," RJ's mother said.

"Yes Mom," RJ frowned.

"But can we still have pizza?" Joey asked hopefully.

RJ's parents and Joey's mother laughed.

"Yes, you can still have pizza," his mother said and grinned at RJ.

Chapter 11

When Saturday night came around, Joey could barely stand still. He was so excited about their pizza night. RJ picked him up at his apartment, and they walked over to Tony's restaurant. He opened early just for them. He had an extra large pizza waiting for them.

"You guys helped out the whole neighborhood," he said as he sat the pizza down in front of them. "This pizza is on the house. But remember, your first job is to keep yourselves safe, hm?" he raised an eyebrow.

"Yes Tony," they both said with a smile. Joey had a very tall glass of orange soda. As they munched on their pizza RJ couldn't stop smiling.

"See, I am a real detective," he said as he took a bite of his pizza.

"Sure you are," Joey said with a grin as he took a sip of his orange soda. "But maybe next time we can eat before we play detective."

"I wasn't playing," RJ insisted and then sighed. "Yes Joey," he agreed. "Next time we'll make sure we eat."

"And," Joey narrowed his eyes as he leaned across the table. "I get two glasses of orange soda!"

"Just this once," RJ agreed with a nod. He hoped that whatever mystery they solved next, it would involve a little less running around as he was exhausted.

Next Steps

I really hope that you've enjoyed this collection of stories and I'd love to hear from you. Please do stop by and let us know how you are enjoying the books!

You can join RJ's fun Facebook page for young detectives here:

https://www.facebook.com/RJBoyDetective

I very much appreciate your reviews and comments so thank you in advance for taking a moment to leave one for "RJ - Boy Detective Books 1-8."

Sincerely,
PJ Ryan

Visit the author website for a complete list of all titles available.

PJRyanBooks.com

CPSIA information can be obtained
at www.ICGtesting.com
Printed in the USA
LVHW04s1721240818
587635LV00003B/253/P